Toilet Bowl Soup
*THE HOLY SH*T*

D1606695

Also by MIKE ADAMS

*Toilet Bowl Soup: Redneck Tales from the Armpit of
America*
A Postcard From A Dead Girl
When the Vomit Makes You Famous
Syringe Songs

Toilet Bowl Soup
*THE HOLY SH*T*

MIKE ADAMS

MA PUBLISHING
SOUTHERN INDIANA

Mike Adams

Mike Adams, his writings and performances are all part of Mike Adams
Publishing of Evansville, Indiana .

ISBN-13: 978-1456513979
ISBN-10: 1456513974

The Holy Sh*t

TO ELAINA AND PATTON

Mike Adams

The Holy Sh*t

In Eastbourne it is healthy
And the residents are wealthy
It's a miracle that anybody dies;
Yet this pearl of English lidos
Is a slaughter house of widows –
If their bank rolls are above the normal size.
If they're lucky in addition
In their choice of a physician
And remember him when making out their wills
And bequeath their Rolls Royces
Then they soon hear angel voices
And are quickly freed from all their earthly ills.
If they're nervous or afraid of
What a heroine is made of
Their mentality will soon be reconditioned
So they needn't feel neglected
They will shortly be infected
With the heroin in which they are deficient.
As we witnessed the deceased borne
From the stately homes of Eastbourne
We are calm, for it may safely be assumed
That each lady that we bury - In the local cemetery
Will re-surface – when the body is exhumed.
It's the mortuary chapel
If they touch an Adam's apple
After parting with a Bentley as a fee
So to liquidate your odd kin
By the needle of the bodkin
Send them down to sunny Eastbourne by the sea.

- John Bodkin Adams
from "Adam and Eves"

PRAISE FOR
TOILET BOWL SOUP
THE HOLY SH*T

"Toilet Bowl Soup is a good read for Hellbilly blood!"
-HANK WILLIAMS III
(Assjack, Superjoint Ritual, Arson Anthem)

"Adams conjures Lautréamont and Bataille yet writes in a
language that only makes sense here, today. It is demented,
post-apocalyptic surrealist prose at its finest. An imagination
that can only be sustained by the dark horrors that feed it.
You will be confused and enlightened."
-TREVOR DUNN
(Bassist & Composer for Mr. Bungle, Fantomas, The Trevor Dunn
Convulsant, John Zorn, and many more)

"Mike Adams has captured the essence of nouveau white-
trash Americana with morbidly delicious imagery. This is
the real thing! It should be required reading for every New
Yorker & Los Angeleno."
- BILLY SHEEHAN
(Bassist for Talas, David Lee Roth, Mr. Big, Niacin, & Steve Via)

"I don't like reading, but I like reading Mike Adams. He's
addictive, brutal and delicious!"
- STEVE BALDERSON
(Writer and director of Pep Squad, Firecracker, Phone Sex, Watch Out,
and Stuck)

"Some of the most amazing, graphic, imaginative, writing I've read in years, fuckin awesome..."
- NEIL WHARTON
(Son of legendary Motley Crue vocalist Vince Neil)

"Mike Adams...What the hell?"
- SCOTT H. BIRAM
(Bloodshot Records recording artist)

"A spectacular combination of humor and borderline insanity of living in Indiana. Strange Tales from a strange state indeed. A must read for everyone!"
- SOLOMON MORTAMUR
(Writer and director of It Came from Trafalgar)

"The ultimate in kinky toilet sex... it makes me proud to be a white trash debutante!"
- GINGER COYOTE
(Vocalist for The White Trash Debutantes and editor of Punk Globe Magazine)

"Adams is one of the most interesting authors of the post 666 generation!"
-SATANIC PANIC MAGAZINE

"I've never been so disturbed and so enlightened at the same time. Adams is truly ahead of his time. The world may not be ready..."
-ROD CASTRO
(Los Angeles based composer who has written music for A&E shows including Gene Simmons Family Jewels, The Two Coreys, LA Ink.)

Mike Adams

Toilet Bowl Soup
*THE HOLY SH*T*

THE WARNING LABEL

The Holy Sh*t was written under the pure unadulterated influence and abuse of the "Farmhouse Cocktail", which on any given day may or may not include four or more of the following: Adderall, Xanex, Lortab, Busch Light, Tacos, Royalty Checks, Heavy Metal and more Groupie Hooker Sex than one man should be entitled to in his lifetime.

This book definitely contains subliminal messages, codes, and other random traces of psychosis. The Holy Sh*t is filled with spelling and grammatical errors, because editors are expensive and editing is fucking boring. Readers should handle this document using extreme caution under black lighting. It is to be advised that the paper in which this book is printed may or may not contain traces of animal fibers, methamphetamines, semen, and whatever pussy juice is made of… There are made up words throughout this document. Fucking deal with it!

Caution… This is not Redneck Tales from the Armpit of America. If you purchased this book hoping for more of that shit, you fucked up!

If you have already found yourself offended by the humble offerings contained herein, you should probably discontinue use immediately and go fuck yourself!

Mike Adams

www.toiletbowlsoup.com

Toilet Bowl Soup: The Holy Sh*t was written between May
2008 – January 2011 in various hotel rooms across America
and in the Warrenton Road Farmhouse.
Written by Mike Adams
Edited by Kat Mykals
Cover Design by MA Publishing
Publicist: James Hoon
Sales: Warren Mackey

Mike Adams writes using Apple Computers, CVS
Composition Notebooks, Hotel Stationery, Ouija Boards, and
Human Blood.

Special Thanks to: John Rauch, Jeremy & Brittney Caine,
Brick Briscoe, Kat Mykals, Brian Adams, Winter Hayden,
Dave & Mary Adams, Kim Ford, Alexandria Moore, Martha
Caine, Steve Balderson, Trevor Dunn, Mike Patton, Little
Ceasars (Pizza, Pizza), Taco Bell, Gary Fullerton, Gator
Mason, Rod Castro, Tom Sizemore, Shannon Hoon, Jim
Morrison, and THE FANS!

The Introduction

Don Corn, drummer for The Charlie Manson Jr. Daniels Band was recently quoted on The Dave Davis Show saying: "if you don't like Mike Adams, it's because you don't know him." I don't believe anyone has captured a more astute truth about someone. He is known by many, or at least many know of him. To know him truly is to love him, (or at least love to hate him). In fact, people who have known both of us at some point in our lives are surprised at the magnitude of our friendship. I assume this stems from the fact that he is vastly misunderstood. Don't get me wrong, the rumors about Mike Adams are usually true. It's astounding that he is still alive given some of the maniacal things he has done. He has spent a considerable amount of his adult life testing any and all kinds of limits. He may not reside on the edge, but he is most certainly a frequent flier.

My first memories of Mike Adams consist of my friends and me eagerly anticipating his band's performances. I was their biggest fan and completely infatuated with their bass player [Adams]. Although I have since grown out of that formerly held infatuation, I am still truly a fan of Mike Adams and his works. I have also come to depend on our friendship for many reasons. He has on more than one occasion pulled me out of a fire (not just metaphorically either). And although someday I won't need the occasional rescue (we hope), I will still depend on him; especially for the enthrallingly infinite conversations that we have. Although we are usually both set in our (usually opposite) ways, we are both receptive to views that conflict with our own. It is often educational and entertaining to say the least.

As an artist, Mike Adams is truly admirable. I encourage his fans to learn about all of the hardships he has endured in order to continue to give birth to brilliantly original productions of a multitude of different facets. The combination of diligence and prowess that he possesses is bound to create a work that has a profound affect on many, (and offend an equal amount as well). He is a true, worn-out sleeveless flannel wearing, blue-collared, Busch light drinking, cranked out redneck. No matter what direction his life may take, those traits will always remain constants of Mike Adams. He will, however, never be content with the daily grind. His mind simply is not built for a repetitive state of normalness. He may be small town, but he is certainly not small minded.

I suggest you do not ask Mike Adams for his opinion unless you truly want it. He is notoriously candid and brutally honest. He has an enormous amount of energy that extends beyond the realm of this metaphysical world. He will definitely live on once his earthly body is laid to rest. In regards to his artistic pursuits, he is truly unprecedented. Many narrow-minded conservative readers will find him distasteful, evil, and even racist, (read it again Oprah). This is simply because Mike Adams, (the man, his work, and his life), is truly an anomaly.

-   KIMBERLY FORD

HOTEL & SUITES
HOLIDAY INN HOTEL AND SUITES
8787 REEDER RD
OVERLAND PARK, KS 66214
Phone: (913) 888-8440
Fax: (913) 888-3438

THE AUTHOR'S NOTE
Starving the Lamb:
The First Wisdom of Madness

Writing a book is a lot like being incarcerated; trapped within the depths of the looming, stark white asylum inside your mind - just trying like ALL be damned to focus both eye & mind underneath a pore - drained psyche, induced by a fucking sick joke called florescent lighting... No man, woman, child or beast possesses the ability to GET sane while being thrashed by the most unholy of light. Blindness would be kinder...

I have been locked away in this goddamn farm house for months; leaving home ONLY for tacos, beer, and a monthly visit to the pharmacy to have my amphetamines & xanex refilled... cannot miss a single dose - cannot write in rehab (fluorescent lighting) Last summer had me spun into a cyclonic hellitorium that laid on top of me with extreme paranoia, one extremely bitter fucking relationship, family, plagues of violence, self loathing, hatred and near suicide... the most lucid psychosis of a

15

serial killer's wet dream.

My sacrificial madness led me into a
ritualistic tremor, 12-14 hour days and
nights; non-stop tourettes style typing;
writing, rewriting - beginning again and
again... I consumed only lethal doses of
medication, Mt. Dew and various concoctions
of brew, with the only true sustenance, a
slice of bologna on left over heels which
were devoured after the speed began showing
signs of slow and my feeding tube of hops
and barley bludgeoned me into a semi-
diabetic coma. All within the remnants of
one mean fucking starvation army. The weight
of the wood - a collective of FORTY POUNDS
lost. Indeed - I dwell within the golden
years of the most rotten.

So where were we? Ah yes, writing books. It
is absolute lunacy. No one in their right
mind should ever embark on such a project
without balls big enough to risk losing
everything; to lose ALL that is and ever was
YOU as a human being. The shell remains
intact, but the mind scrapes the bottom of
something theoretically bottomless. Most
people will quickly jump aboard - all of
them dressed out in a variety of pseudo-
fashion without carefully considering what
it actually means to voyage beyond sight of
land on a sinking ship. These people are
nothing but Hemmingway cliché's attempting
to support some supposed symmetry between
talent and psychosis. I am not speaking of
the psychosis that so many believe they have
obtained through bouts of simple misery or
loss of comfort. I am speaking in terms of a

word that cannot be articulated or translated. The pitch is unrecognizable, but it can be felt deep inside the smallest cavity of the mind. This madness is not madness; it is not fashionable depression. It is unexplainable, and it only exists through decades of excessive damage... Irreparable Goddamages.

I will speak no more of this. Those of you who understand need no further explanation (as you nod your head in agreement). When I am not wasting my time valuably, I spend most of my days writing in long-wind; constructing a series of one-liners and phrases, which will likely never be deciphered and understood by anyone, including me. All of them began as a single fire, now an inferno of words and agendas that I no longer control. Perhaps I haven't had control of them from the inception. Ideas are under estimated and so many are taken for granted - moments of clarity and superior wisdom, wasted on countless pleasures & killers of time beginning and ending with _____ (fill in the blank).

Remember, this is only a note from a supposed maniac - just a man sharing a single day with its light and darkness smeared across his sleeve. For me, this is cheaper than therapy and undoubtedly more effective. With that being said, I leave you with this… Do not try this at home!

"Rothchild is not your father…I am."
—The Terrorvision of the Seven December
(XXI)

There are some scientists who theorize that
the sun will utilize the capacity of its
hydrogen within the next five billion years,
thus rendering its illumination to a void.
The sun will then swell to that of a red
giant before the withering outer layers fade
away, emerging a pale star. An interesting
theory, and an even more interesting
metaphor for the lives that all of us stars
choose to lead, the starts we choose to
believe in, the colors, the shapes, the
size, the magnitude of what our lifetime has
to offer,and our denial in self regression.

We are a declining population. Everything
must move from left to right before we dare
see it. Even when it remains understood, It,
All, both Fact and Fiction, must first
trickle down stream to create awareness. WE
THE PEOPLE must literally witness the cesspool
rush across our bare feet before complaining
about standing in shit.

This is your world; a retarded populous
breathing in what is out there without
knowing, disregarding the many messages from
the heavens, while carrying the weight of

the wood across a straight line life desert
journey into the first gate of hell. We use
these illusions that have manifested in
order to feel comfortable rather than happy.
Yet, these perverse programming efforts of
the generations have passed on a consensus
that happiness can only be obtained by
avoiding chaos as opposed to living inside
of it.

We…us…me…YOU live through the varying
degrees of this mirage of progress and
responsible evolution, leaving us well
enough for dead with little to no growth.
All of this time is spent inside of these
circles spinning ourselves into a
neurological state of the dizziest regret,
absolute fear, and remorseful melancholy. To
eat from this spiritual wasteland is to
devour emptiness from a land filled chalice
full of countless lost and unclaimed souls
who have missed every opportunity to see all
of their own missed opportunities. They
exist inside of every slumber, idea, song
and dance. For the stars to live as they
were programmed to live is to live unloved
by those who continue to run the code, deep
inside THE HOLY SHIT.

The American empire is nearing its end, and
the words of others have bitten off more
than they can chew. Isn't that how it always
seems to go? Human nature fades the soul
from the womb, but the ego, the size of our
heads gets bigger, dumber, less efficient.
Yet no matter how much of this is true I
somehow continue. Maybe it is a lot of luck,
or maybe just a little understanding, but

one thing is for sure - within these four
walls, I am the biggest legend that ever
lived.

THE LOCUST THEORY
Part I: Mechanical Maggots

I found myself standing in the middle of a room in a house full of grey people who appeared to be dying off one by one, slipping into a seemingly deep hibernation phase after an ambitious attempt to make the most of wasted time. From where I was standing, through the countless episodes of sporadic strobe like flashes and recurring momentary blindness, all human consciousness had been viciously chewed and spit out through unforeseen tail spins of emotional release and psychological breakdown. Those of us able to face our demons were left holding our brown decomposing hearts within the palms of our hands, as we fought to reconnect with those missing pieces that had committed our souls to this institution; molting with hopes of emerging into new life, and leaving behind those elements of the past that were no longer needed.

I proceeded to contemplate a theory, one placing an individual's depth and ability to recognize complex emotion, as well as the ability to develop unique perceptions. By challenging and conquering the psyche to the point of atrophy, the individual would then be able to shed mental disfigurements. I wrote it down *The Locust Theory*.

The voice of a little boy spoke to me... Close by. I spun around to see who it was but saw nothing except slabs of junkies in the coldest slumber. The boy continued speaking. The sound of his voice penetrated deep inside my left ear, shifted densely to the right, leaving behind a disabling high pitched tone. The chimes planted inside of my ear were in flames, and my jugular pulsated overwhelming sensations of red all over the right side of my face. I took a deep breath and pondered the probability of having a stroke while coming down off amphetamines. I had never heard of such a thing. Underneath The Locust Theory I wrote: some locusts may die before molting is complete?

"What was this?" I thought to myself. "Was this a legitimate experiment?" "Why was I conducting it?" I didn't understand where the motivation was coming from. My memory, as well as simple understanding were beginning to fail, disintegrating from profound chalkboard equations into useless dust. If I closed my eyes I could envision what I wanted to think about, but couldn't interpret structure, shape, meaning, or words. It was a hazy looking glass; a world at the tip of my tongue. Existence block.

The young boy began speaking again, his voice resonating inside of my ears like termites trying to tune a symphony of

transistor radios. The noise was disabling,
yet curious as I was able to make out pieces
of what he was saying.
"Where are you?" I asked, as the boy
desperately persisted. The more I tried to
focus on what he was asking, the less sense
I was able to make of it.
"Where are you?" I asked again. "I can't
understand what you are saying. What do you
want?" My ear was now consistently ringing
consistently, and upon laying my hand over
it for comfort, I realized it was seeping
blood from its core. Prying around inside of
it to determine a cause, I asked myself,
"What causes an ear to bleed?"

The boy was now shouting frantically, but no
matter how hard I tried, I still couldn't
understand. The tone of his voice had me
disoriented and it frightened me beyond that
of simple fear. It was like an infinity of
mechanical maggots, razor sharp larva with a
unique odor, and a life of their own, eating
away at pieces of me I had never felt. I
cicled the room, moving over top of
furniture cluttered with bodies, ashtrays,
and empty bottles of beer, trying to see the
voice… hear a boy.

I felt the room change shades. Light was not
functional and what appeared to be shadows
were just lingering souls forcing their way
inside of anything they could, but couldn't…
I was knee deep in a zombie pile. The house
was a cocoon for the undead. There were
riots of movement going on behind me. I spun
around - nothing but moulting zombies.

The voice of the boy was now beginning to
sound more emotionally charged and violent.
At times, a haunting silence sealed the room
increasing awareness of my rapid heartbeat,
face of fire, and inability to breathe. A
plastic bag, duct tape, adrenalin, anxiety,
but no death. I was being tortured. With my
ear still bleeding, I wondered how long it
would take before the pile of zombies
surrounding me would resurrect and pull me
into hell. Death would be better than this.
The killing frequency was in Morris code,
pitched at deafening heights, turning my
body into crooked stone, and tightly locking
my eye lids shut, severing my brains ability
to communicate voluntarily and
involuntarily. This was undead…

I kicked a few of the monsters lying on the
floor, receiving no response. Looking at
myself in a mirror behind a green screen. I
was not one of them. Not yet. I had somehow
overcome the infection, but couldn't
understand where it had come from. The only
signs of life that remained were me and the
voice of a boy whom I had been communicating
with but couldn't focus on clearly. Maybe he
was a ghost… an angel… a demon… No matter
what he said, I couldn't believe it.
Sometimes children pull molting locusts from
the tree before the process is complete. I
wrote it down.
"Could the boy be the source of infection?"
I thought to myself, confused, trying to
piece it together in an attempt to defend
myself against what had happened to the
others. No matter how much I tried to
dissect what was going on around me, through

scattered reductive reasoning, I couldn't
make any distinction between the light and
dark areas. It could be aliens committing
insanity assaults on the human race using
frequencies carrying torture cells. Succumb
and live. Deny and perish.

My thoughts continued to scatter, shifting
toward the startling possibility that the
lifeless souls spread around the room were
not zombies at all… but people I had
murdered. "Goddamnit did I?" I asked staring
down at the floor… nothing but corpses,
lifeless, visually examining some of them
for blood or bruising, but fearing infection
from the slightest contact. Confusion set
in. Was I the Killer or just immune? "Why
would zombies unify and molt?" I thought to
myself, then I quickly answered my own
question, "Zombies do not moult."

The incomprehensive shrieks and hysterics of
the little boy's voice incessantly piercing
through my weary mind were torturing me to
the point of wanting to end my life. My face
was still burning…impending stroke, zombie
sodomy, a common cold, north or south? I
laughed a lot and then cried and then seized
up and laughed again… crying, crying,
nothing - calm.

I perused the room for a gun. No more fear…
scarred as hell. "I murdered tonight," I
thought to myself. "A" is "Z" and "Y" is
somewhere between the ears, bleeding still.
"Bleeding," I yelled aloud, needing very
much to escape the greyest grave buried
within the universe. The voice wasn't a boy

at all but a serpent. These were zombie serpents… undead strikers, venomous constrictors. I unlocked the unhinged door facing swallowing a lump of death before stepping outside.

Part II: The Dueling Suns of the Continuum

The sun was coming up in the distance, patiently illustrating the day through the cracks of my desert worn eyes. A future worth of children lay dying in each other's arms. All victims and liars, violent grins and attempted murder; a street in line with the devil, unaware of a poison cocoon dictated by an unseen serpent plotting a holocaust, the second coming. No Christ is risen through the eyes of this day. A dead land, a dead language, morality and penance were for nothing. Inside the hollow Siamese eyes, a continuum… It was sadomasoschitzophrenic… A place where nothing being savored for purposes of destruction and euphoria has ever existed. No fabric or disguise… No opinion… No song. My legs were dead, weak, and exhausted. Like steel with elasticity, I made every attempt to dredge on through the quicksand graveyard, dodging a slow motion reign of thousands of razor blades being cast down by an unmerciful Maple, a wooden soldier trained to kill anything that emerged from the cocoon. My eyes were sewn tight while I gripped my hands around my neck to prevent being sliced across the jugular. It was a fight between the elements and inexperience

as I made every attempt to get to my car
without being cut in half or swallowed. The
car was unlocked. I dove into the driver's
seat just before the wooden soldier
scattered another thousand blades across the
yard. All of my surroundings were facing
east. The sun was rising over both ends of
the earth. Doomsday was here.

I could feel my eyes rolling around freely
inside of my skull. It was the fiercest case
of lazy eye conceivable. My head was
positioned to look forward yet one eye
seemed to be aimed at my crotch and the
other into the backseat. I began rubbing the
sockets vigorously with the palms of my
hands resulting in a kaleidoscope of
posterior vitreous detachment… I was seeing
stars. I cocked my head slightly to the
right, squinting to my clearest perception,
trying to turn the ignition switch. I
couldn't calculate how to make the goddamned
thing roll… move. I could see the pattern;
engage clutch, turn ignition, (flash of
floaters), put into 1st gear, (flash of my
throat being cut), slowly release the
clutch, (flash of me drowning), accelerate,
engage clutch, (flash of being shot in the
head), shift into 2nd, (flash of
masturbating slit wrist), and so on… My mind
was racing, hyper madness; lazy eyes,
potential pandemic, murder, and infection.
"Why did I kill all of those people?" I
thought to myself while side winding across
the yard and through a three foot ditch that
launched the car into the street on the way
out of town. The car began hopping up and
down chirping like a flaming nest full of

precocial hatchlings. I found myself in and
out of consciousness. I was brought to by
flashing visions of my own suicide in slow
motion... looking down the barrel, feeling
the shell enter the roof of my mouth and
excruciating pain as pieces of my head began
to fly apart, killing me slowly. I had to
get someplace safe… I was the last person
seen alive running out of a house full of
death.

WELCOME TO
THE BROWN EYE BAR & GRILL

There is a twist of fate hovering above the lives of those both mangy and wild. It is those two legged breeders who continue the shit dance inside the shifting circles of deformity and retardation. They come in packs, communities; watch for them. These rats crumble slowly around each other; decrepit are these monsters' stability, yet they pose with such brutish vigor, like diseased trees, naked and erect, arms outstretched with degenerate boner lust, eating themselves from the inside out. These crippled beasts teeter on the sharpest edge of simple death, dwelling underneath the same pissmal grey skies. Some of them jack off with banana peels, while the majority simply lingers within the stench, slobbering on the skin of their next meal. Some of you may digest this society that I am speaking to you about as a cult, but truth be told, it is more of a dung menagerie, looming within a poignant skanktamoneous oblivion. You can choose to ignore them, you can choose not to care, but no matter how furious the battle this abominable, spermicidal populous cannot be killed. Not by me, not by you!

In a place like this the day is best spent trying to forget about it, usually getting piss yourself drunk inside one of the local taverns. I preferred a little place downtown just off Locust Street called Fullerton's Tavern America. A quiet little shotgun type bar, it's a fine place to chase away the morning dew with cheap beer, and if your timing is right, a couple of dry pancakes to soak it all up.

Ol' Gary Fullerton, the son-of-a-bitch who owned the goddamned place, opened somewhere around nine in the morning. Although, if Gary thought you were good shit, you could beat on the back door like a bad dog somewhere around eight. If he was already up and at it, he'd let you in early just to keep the neighbors from raising hell. You would think you really pissed him off because after a couple of knocks you could hear Gary shouting some shit like, "You cross-eyed son of a mother's cunt." This just before jerking the door off its hinges, standing in the doorway wearing nothing but his white boxer shorts and a pair of black dress socks pulled up around the fat of his calves. He never seemed to care once he realized that it was me beating his door down, but then again, I always tried to be respectful. I did my best not to abuse his generosity. I didn't want that bastard to ever turn me away on a day when I really needed a morning drunk.

I. Gary Fullerton
The Diplomatic Alcoholic

Gary was the kind of guy who should have been mid-life by the time he was nineteen or twenty. All I ever saw that motherfucker eat was pork rinds with a bourbon chaser. He had a vile temper, but he was also a really good guy…a pillar of the community in most people's eyes. The Tavern America served up some of the best food in town, and among other things, was a key sponsor for just about everything from little league to the special olympics. Gary ran a pretty tight ship, and did a good amount of business because of it. He kept all of the typical bar bullshit that usually breeds in that type of place to a minumum. Anytime some asshole decided to get belligerent in front of Gary's *respectable* lunch crowd, his face would turn devil red, and yet, he always handled the situation very diplomaticly. Most of the time he'd just politely and quietly ask the asshole to leave, and if they didn't leave on their own, Gary would personally walk them to the door with his arm wrapped firmly around their necks as if he was walking with an old friend. Usually, the other customers were completely oblivious to what was going on. Gary was just that fucking good at asshole removal, but for those of us who did know, we knew that through Gary's red faced, diplomatic smile that he was whispering some mafia noise like, "Pull that type of shit in here again and I'll have you butchered and bronzed cocksucker". Once Gary got the asshole outside, he'd usually end it by saying something like, "Come on by later tonight and we'll discuss your manners son." Some nights the asshole would show. Some nights he wouldn't. Those who didn't come around for a while had likely sobered up, realized how much of an asshole they had been, and made the wise decision to put some distance between them and the Tavern America for awhile. Those assholes who showed up later to discuss their manners with Gary usually wound up getting a sawed off mop handle smashed across their face. I mean he'd nearly pull his arm out of socket giving them an old fashion nigger beatdown before choking them out and tossing them in the dumpster… "You little cocksucker. Consider yourself fucking barred cocksucker. If I see your little monkey fuck face in here again motherfucker, I'll kill your fucking tits!"

I've always considered Gary a good friend of mine, and I'm relatively sure he thinks the same of me. He knows I can be trusted and most of the time that is a good enough quality to have in someone you call a friend. Now, even though Gary conducted himself with a certain political protocol around most of the town's people, he wasn't a saint by any stretch of the imagination.

Gary was a thoroughbred alcoholic, but one of the most stable of the breed. He could, and from what I've seen, he did drink liquor all night, every night…but aside from his words shifting more towards the vulgar, you could never tell he had been drinking. He was a true professional – "booze only, no fucking dope!", he would say nearly every time I was around him. Gary was from the old school, one who adimantly damns the use of all illegal drugs because he believes they have nothing but a negative influence on young people. He blamed illegal drugs, or "fucking dope" as he often put it, for the degeneration of modern society…all with the exception of marijuana.

Gary didn't believe marijuana should be illegal, but he always handled the subject with a certain predjudice and selective secrecy. Meaning, if you ever felt like discussing the politics surrounding the legalization or decriminalization of marijuana with him, you had to wait for him to initiate the conversation. In his mind, certain subject matter could easily compromise his upstanding community relations, as well as make him a target. So if Gary decided he could trust you with his ideas and opinions, he would always make it perfectly clear that everything he said or did after hours within the confines of the Tavern America or his upstairs apartment; everything, all of it was to be considered a solemn secret and taken to the grave.

Some nights, just after last call, Gary would walk around, giving a select few a

round of free beer just to stick around
after closing and help him clean up. Nothing
difficult; just restocking the coolers,
taking out a few bags of trash and
depending on the night, maybe spot mopping a
blood stain off the floor. There was usually
no more than thirty minutes worth of work
before the lights were out and the doors
locked. Afterwards, we'd follow Gary
upstairs to his apartment which was
conveniently located above the bar.

If you got high with Gary you could always
count on being up there for hours, listening
to his high speed rants and tales of his
life told through an old stoner perspective.
One night I heard him say, "I've never met a
stoner rapist" followed shortly thereafter
by, "Smoking pot never gave anybody AIDS."
This much was true. Ol' Gary wore his
convictions on his sleeve much like a wild
animal gnashing its teeth seconds after its
release from captivity. "A little booze, a
little weed, but all that other shit will
have you suckin' cock and homeless."

II. Gary Fullerton
The Pot Head Patriot

Stoner Gary was as much of a pseudo historian as he was actually paranoid. He would constantly use misinterpretations of history as the basis of his knowledge and beliefs in early America. There was a certain level of bug-eyed confidence that crawled out of the sockets of his mind as he waved us all in just a little closer right before whispering something like, *"You know what? The foundation of this nation's goddamned government was conceived by men just like us. You know, men who not only smoked marijuana, but grew it in abundance. Yes sir, our forefathers, hell they gave us something pretty goddamned good in the beginning. They gave us the right to carry guns. Hell, they even gave us the right to remain silent. This free country of ours was supposed to be a lot simpler, but now, well now all of these coon clit bureaucrats got their fuckin hands and ears in everything we do. They've got fucking surveillance positioned everywhere son. There are cameras everywhere from grocery store parking lots right down to the goddamned ladies room."*

Even though Gary was a bit of a conspiracy theorist, he was not entirely wrong… just somewhat skewed, but mostly just paranoid. One night after we all got really fucking high he told me that he believed that local officials like the Fire Marshall and Health Inspector were actually government

operatives. He said, "I just know those ass
gaskets are in there planting and rotating
bugs every time they pull one of those
goddamned surprise inspections." I didn't
know what to think, or even what to say to
him. I usually just agreed with him, most of
the time saying something like, "You know
what Gary, that's entirely fucking possible
man." A comment like that had him on the
prowl. I remember sitting at the bar one
evening, and from out of nowhere my nerves
were being rattled by what sounded like
someone hurling pots and pans at a rat
across the kitchen. To the others who had
just been startled by the same chaos, to
them, the noise probably sounded like a
dishwasher had just busted his ass… but I
knew what was really going on. Gary got all
wrapped up in his paranoia and momentarily
snapped, tearing his kitchen apart trying to
find a bug.

It was always amusing to just sit back and
listen to him carry on and on about "the
downtrodden of uncivil society" and "hairy
wrecking balls against the foundation" type
of shit. I enjoyed antagonizing him,
teetering on his exposed nerves, creating a
human live wire. All I ever had to do was
add some random footnote to one of his
rants. I'd say something like, "Hey man, did
you know that Thomas Edison was strung out
on cocaine, morphine and even strychnine
while trying to invent the light bulb?" Man!
Old Gary's eyes would blow straight through
the top of his head. He'd get all pissed-
the-fuck-off and shout, "Bull-fuckin-shit!",

jumping around like a seizure looking for a home. "Your history book is missin some fuckin' pages son! There ain't no way! There ain't no goddamned fuckin way! I've been around a lot of dopers in my time and there aint no goddamned way any of those bastards could ever invent a fuckin light bulb!" To watch him come alive was like watching Tennessee Meat trying to mount a restless breed of Nubian goat. There was a lot of commotion and heavy breathing, but it all fell just a few inches short of getting inside of the fucking point. A man like Gary could never begin to fathom, much less believe in, the idea of one of the greatest inventions of all time having been conceived and manifested by a man under the influence of speed, pain killers, and rat poison. For guys like Gary, easily swallowed ideas and opinions were best. A man like him needed to hold on to a faith in the theory that all great minds and people produced all great things… and that all of the greatest people, with the greatest minds, did not, and would not ever use hard drugs to assist them in becoming great.

III. Sweet Mary Hell
Callaway Axe & The Ol' Adderall Eye

Even the fuckin' dumbest fuckin' redneck
knows that you cannot just walk onto some
farmer's property and steal his mule. No
sir! There is some serious legwork that any
good animal thief must endure before
attempting a heist. In this case my brother,
Brian, got mixed up with a psychotic gang of
satanic Hispanics led by The Brothers
Chavez. These guys didn't have to do half
the shit they did in order to make a living.

They owned two Mexican restaurants within a
half mile of each other, both of them packed
every fucking night. Of course, these
fucking spics couldn't do anything on the up
and up… they got fuckin' bored. The entire
fuckin' gang was more vicious than any wild
fucking animal… even a goddamned rabid
elchupacabra would tuck tail and haul ass
after being beat with a ball bat wrapped in
bloody rags soaked in turpentine, but these
motherfuckers.

One night after a fuck load of tequila and a
chimichanga chaser, that dumb fuck brother
of mine makes friends with these guys. After
they shacked him up in the Valley Court
Trailer Park, got him cranked out of his
fuckin' mind, promised him a piñata, and let
him bang some skanky little gutter whores to
the Tijuana Brass… That fucker promised them
a mule.

So there we were… Planning to steal a donkey for these bendechos, a task that had to be handled with kid gloves, because of course, not just any four legged ass would do. It goes without saying, but if we fucked up and stole a donkey that didn't meet the spics' specifications, we would run the risk of not selling the goddamned thing. Then we'd be stuck holding a borrowed mule, so to speak.

To do a job like this right, you have to first locate some prospects, photograph them without being captured or killed, and then present them to the prospective buyer, allowing them to pick from a photo lineup. A good ol' fashion donkey heist is a two man job. Don't ever let anyone tell you differently. Add more people than that to your crew, and not only do you cut into your profits, but your odds of getting caught increase well beyond the largest risk involved. You're going to need a digital camera. Not one of those easy share pieces of shit either… you want to store your photos on a memory card, not directly onto your camera. This way you can get rid of the evidence that you took any fucking pictures of a dumbass donkey. You're also going to need some heavy, someone like my crazy-ass brother, to feed the beast handfuls of shredded carrots while holding a loaded fucking pistol pressed firmly against its head. The carrots are usually enough to keep a donkey still during a barnyard photo shoot... The pistol is a literal kill switch. No matter what, if the mule gets spooked and starts all his buckin' and hee-

hawin around, you've got no choice but to
lay that fucker down with a single bullet to
the brain.

Most of the time the carrots are enough to
keep the beast calm, but you never really
know how the animal will react until the
second immediately following the first flash
of the camera. You've always got to go
prepared for the worst, just like anything
involving probability and farm animals. Most
times, the goddamned animal just stood there
like it's posing for a fuckin' glamour shot,
but every now and then, just as you're
crawlin' around in a thick mix of mud and
donkey shit, bitchin' to your partner,
saying something like, "Why am I always the
one crawling around in this shit, taking
snapshots of donkey dicks?" The donkey
sneezed. There's no buckin or hee-hawin', no
fury vicious enough to cripple either one of
us, just a sneeze…and then it happened…
BANG!

"Goddamn!" I shouted. "God-fucking-damn!"
The blood filled my eyes. I was literally
choking on donkey brains, and aside from
blindness and throwing up the cerebral
cortex of a jackass with an allergic
reaction. The sound of the pistol had
deafened me. After I rubbed the blood out of
my eyes, I could see the look of terror on
my brother's face. His lips were moving, but
I couldn't hear a fucking thing. There was
just a ringing in my ears, a tone like a
test from the Emergency Broadcasting System
reverberating inside of my fucking skull.

Brian was waving a smoking gun around in my face as if he was attempting to pistol whip some kind of redneck sign language. I didn't get it. I was disoriented. I felt like Helen Keller waking up from a nap in a fuckin' slaughterhouse.

The two of us ran for dear life, leaving the headless ass behind. We jumped into the truck and kicked ass out of there, burning down the road at top speed without our headlights on.

"What the fuck just happened?" I asked my brother, trying to get some fucking clue as to what exactly provoked him to execute that goddamned mule.

"Are you out of your goddamn mind? You nearly killed me back there. I mean, what the fuck?"

"He fuckin made a move," my brother replied.

"A move?" I shouted, "It fucking sneezed Brian!"

"All I know is the motherfucker tried to bite my motherfuckin' hand off."

"You fuckin' watched the 'Reservoir Dogs' today didn't you?" I asked. "Because something got you acting like motherfuckin' Mr. Pink back there!"

"Mr. Blonde," my brother replied.

"What the fuck are you talking about?"

"You accused my behavior, which ultimately led to the death of that jackass, of being similar to that of Mr. Pink."

"Yeah, Brian, you're Mr. fucking Pink, and I'm Mr. fucking Grey!"

I wanted to kill him.

"There aint no Mr. Grey in Reservoir Dogs"
my brother replied. "There's a Mr. White, a
Mr. Orange, Blue, Brown, and a Mr. Pink,
played by Steve Buschemi, who fuckin' laid
it down badass. And last but not least,
there is Mr. Blonde, who you have mistaken
for Mr. Pink. There's definitely no fucking
Mr. Grey."
"It's a metaphor you fuckin' ass clown!" I
shouted. "I don't give two fuckin' flying
shits if you're Mr. Pink, Blonde, or Mr.
Nigger Fucking Yellow. Take a good look at
me. This mess, the one that has me covered
in a blanket of jackass brains, is your
mess. You need to get me to a fucking lake."
"Look, I'm fuckin' sorry" my brother
shouted. "What was I suppose to do? As far
as I'm concerned, that bitch hit the fuckin'
alarm button. It's the donkey's fault. He
shouldn't have hit my fuckin' alarm button."
"It fucking sneezed Brian!"
At this point, I was beyond pissed.
"That's not a cause for alarm. The fact that
I'm coughing up bloody jackass brains, now
that, that's a fuckin' alarm button. Mr.
Blonde my aching ass!"
"Fuck you."
"Fuck you! New fuckin' rule, no more fucking
gangster movies before we go to work. I mean
it Brian. No more wise guy shit."
"Look," my brother said to me, trying to
explain his position further. "I did what
you told me to do. Right before we left your
house you said, 'Brian, no matter what, if
the donkey cries, the donkey dies.' Did you
or did you not say those very fuckin'
words?"

"You're the one who said that you fucking cum-quat" I shouted. "I told you if the donkey starts to kick and buck, he's fucked! Nowhere in that statement could any sane person comprehend that as, 'execute the fucking beast, if it fucking sneezes!'" I shook my head.
"You know what? Fuck you man! The whole night is fucked and all you can do is complain about swallowing a few pieces of brain. We've got to get the brothers Chavez a donkey by next Tuesday or I don't even know what's going to happen to us."
"To us? You know what, you're right Brian. The entire night is fucked. In fact, this rudimentary idea of stealing a live fucking animal for these trailer park spics is just about the most fucked up mess you've ever gotten me into. So fuck me… fuck you! I'm not getting paid to eat the brains of your idiot mistakes just so these guys can have a circle jerk, or finger fuck farm animals!"

We had photos of two donkeys, one with its head and one without. It was the best we could do. Now, all my brother had left to do is show the Brothers Chavez what we had and hope the one we hadn't killed was good enough. Then my brother and I could formulate a plan for safely obtaining the donkey without being arrested and charged with theft, animal cruelty, and now thanks to Michael Bessigano, perhaps even bestiality. The entire state of Indiana has been in an uproar since the story of Michael Bessigano hit the papers a few years ago.

Mike Adams

Legislature passes bill outlawing bestiality
NIRPC LOOKS TO GET PAID ON TIME
Story (from Northwest Indiana Times)
PATRICK GUINANE
April 13, 2007

INDIANAPOLIS | Legislation to outlaw sex with animals is on its way to the governor. The recent parole of a man convicted of sexually assaulting and killing a chicken in a Valparaiso motel room sparked the move to make bestiality a distinct crime in Indiana.

Michael Bessigano, 36, received a 10.5-year prison sentence after admitting he stole a farm chicken in May 2001 and took it to a U.S. 30 motel, where he killed the animal while having sex with it.

Bessigano had a history of arrests involving alleged abuse or theft of dogs, geese and a rooster, all of which helped prosecutors secure a maximum sentence for animal cruelty. But prosecutors couldn't charge Bessigano with bestiality.

"For some reason in the recodification -- and no one seems to know why -- in 1977, the offense of bestiality was left off our criminal code," said state Rep. Linda Lawson, D-Hammond.

Lawson sponsored House Bill 1387, which would make a sex act with an animal a misdemeanor punishable by up to a year behind bars and a maximum fine of $5,000. The crime becomes a felony punishable by up to three yeas in prison if the animal "suffers extreme pain or death."

The House voted 85-0 Wednesday to accept minor changes made to the legislation by the Senate. It's now up to Gov. Mitch Daniels to sign or veto the bill.

NIRPC bill advances

The Northwestern Indiana Regional Planning Commission is

just a step away from ensuring it gets paid on time. The House voted 87-0 Thursday to agree with slight revisions the Senate made to House Bill 1595. The legislation, which still must be signed by the governor, would encourage Lake, LaPorte and Porter counties to pay their annual NIRPC dues from income taxes or riverboat casino cash -- anything other than property taxes, which have been slow to arrive in recent years. "Anything that takes away real estate tax as a method of paying for things has got to be good to me," state Rep. Ed Soliday, R-Valparaiso, said in encouraging colleagues to support the measure. If a county wants to stick with property taxes, it would have to document NIRPC's levy on property tax bills, and NIRPC would be allowed to borrow to cover cash flow.

The legislation also would expand NIRPC's executive board from eight to 11 members, giving each county an additional seat.

So there we were again... One morning in early March, my brother and I showed up in the alley behind the Tavern America. It was one hell of a chilly fucking morning. Both of us looked and smelled like we just killed an animal. We reeked of sudden death and the explosive discharge of fifty filthy assholes. We had been out all night long on some sort of a clandistine mission, scouring dimly lit farms far from the beaten path of the well postured, coherent citizens. Our mission was to find a farm with a well hung donkey residing within its confines. We were to steal the beast and then sell it to some wet-back at wholesale.

Drunk and covered in donkey shit, the two of us took turns beating on Gary's back door. We really wanted to get in off the streets and wash up, have a few more beers and do our best to con Ol' Gary into fixing us something to eat. But no matter how much we knocked, he wouldn't answer. We were just about to give up when my brother spotted an old golf club in between a few pieces of rotted plywood and some concrete blocks. "Callaway," he said swinging it like a lanatic at chunks of alley gravel. "I've heard of these. Pretty good clubs."

My brother has never even played golf. I think the closest he ever got to the game was renting a cart after coming down from a four night tweaker binge and course cruising for doctors that he might be able to use as a narcotics connection.
"Let me see that goddamned thing," I said, reaching out for opportunity to turn a silver moment into gold. I lifted the Callaway above my head and began to chop away at the back door like a volunteer fireman with a dull ax. The sound of the club ricocheting off the door was violent, and could probably be heard throughout every goddamned house in town. The brutality of it all got my brother wound up. He was jumping around, hissing and spitting, howling like an alley cat, throwing gravel, and even occasionally groping his crotch as he kicked the dumpster. It wasn't long before we heard the torrential roars of Gary.
"Goddamn a crippled Christ to Hell!" He howled, declaring his insatiable need to

stomp a hole in "queer-fudge" and "mutt-humpers". That motherfucker was trampling full blast toward the door like a fully erect bull. When I heard Gary blazing full throttle down the stairs I began to question my judgment. Gary was shouting, "Who is it? Who's there? What do you want?" All of this was followed by some babbling about not being open until nine o' clock.

A good friend will do one of two things in a situation like this. They will either make an attempt to calm the nervous fat man by revealing themselves, and apologizing for fucking with him so early in the morning…or they will pause for a moment, get into character and push that bucket of lard right over the edge.
"This is the FBI" I shouted, in my deepest authoritative asshole cop voice. "We need to speak to Mr. Gary Fullerton." My brother just stood there, staring at me in complete silence, but with a snydley shit eating grin. We stood as tight as they come. I knew that he knew what was next...

"Ahhh… Who's asking?" Gary replied, his voice shaking, quivering like a timid little girl. Had I actually been a cop I would have immediately believed him to be guilty of whatever it was he was being accused of.
"Sir this is Special Agent Michaels with the Federal Bureau of Investigations", forcing my tone into that of a pissed off Federal Agent who had been up for too many days tracking drug dealers and pornographers, in absolutely no mood to fuck around with some

sleazy bar owner. "We need to question Mr. Fullerton about the exploitation and prostitution of mentally disabled, underage children."

"Prostitution," he screamed. "I ain't been doin' no prostitutin'. You got the wrong fuckin' guy sir."

"Listen motherfucker," I shouted, "I'll decide who's been pimpin' out 'tards and teenagers. Not you! Now let us before we break down this motherfucking door!"

Gary started stuttering around, saying something about how he needed to comb his hair and put on some pants. I beat on the door with that old Calaway even harder, screaming, "Mr. Fullerton! Do not walk away from this door sir. By failing to cooperate with our investigation you are clearly incriminating yourself."

"You got a search warrant?" Gary asked, his voice still shaking like a dog shitting peach seeds.

"I don't need a fucking search warrant to ask questions Mr. Fullerton! But if you really want to play with our balls, we'll get you a fucking warrant within the hour, and then come back here and wipe our asses with it before pulling this piece of shit bar apart. Hell, we'll even put the word out through the local news that the FBI is now closely monitoring this goddamned shit eating dive and its patrons as suspected pedophiles. Do you want to fuck with us like that you miserable, cocksucking, baby raping, son of a bitch!??!"

"I ain't got no children in here mister," Gary cried out like a stuttering faggot who had just swallowed his tongue. "I aint got no whores, grown or otherwise man. I just need to get my pants."

"Mr. Fullerton," I shouted at him aggressively, almost maniacally. "Listen fuck face, my second in command and I now have a couple of 10mm Glock 20's aimed directly at this door. You're acting like a maniac sir and if you do not open this goddamned door, that is enough probable fucking cause for us to kick down this piece of shit with brute fucking force."

"Jesus Mary cunt!" Gary shouted, paranoid to the point of lunacy. His apprehension toward my demands told me that he was likely holding a little weed. In Gary's mind a drug charge, even a misdemeanor, was suicide. "I'll open it. Give me a minute. I'll open the goddamned door. Jesus sons of shit!"

"Whoa-whoa-whoa-whoa-whoa," I said as he fumbled around with a series of latches and locks, working to get the door open before it was sprayed by bullets. "I'm going to need you to unlock that door and open it very fucking slooooowly."

"I told you I'm opening it!" He shouted back with fear clenched in between his teeth.

"Listen to me Mr. Fullerton. List-en…to…me. I've got an extremely anxious partner here who is ready to fire an entire round of bullets straight up your ass if need be.

"I'll rape you with this motherfucker, dead or alive!" my brother shouted. "So after you unlock the door, I'm going to need you to open it just far enough for you to slide those greasy paws of yours outside the door so we can see your fucking hands, and do it

all very fucking slowly – Do you
understand?"
"Sweet Mary hell," Gary snapped back. "Yeah,
yeah, yeah. Just calm down…please."

After he unlocked and unbolted the door,
Gary said "Ok, I'm gonna open it now." He
sounded like a hostage victim seconds from
release, but almost certain he would be shot
in the back once he made a run for it. As
the door began to creep open, I reared back
on the old Callaway. Gary's fat hands slowly
emerged from behind the door. "Is this ok?"
Neither my brother or I said a word. I fired
off a swing from the old Callaway, smashing
the driver as hard as I could against the
door, the part I estimated closest to his
fat head. SSSSPRAAAAAANNNNNK!

What followed was the harsh shrieking of
something not quite human and the rumble of
a three hundred plus pound man being brought
down by sheer terror. He sounded like a
spooked nine-year-old girl at the end of a
scary story being told during a slumber
party. "Jeeezus shit!" He squealed like his
vocal chords had been lubricated with Hot
Damn and burnt fry oil. "You shot me. I
think you shot me. You said you wouldn't
shoot… slooowly, I did slowly. Goddamn…
Goddamn!" When I opened the door Gary was
lying face down on the floor with his hands
locked behind his head. He was wearing one
flip-flop and a large pair of white boxer
briefs with a six inch skid mark down the
crack of his ass. "Gary you fucking choad,"
my brother shouted. "It's just us, fat boy.

Get your ass up. Goddamn man. Are you
fucking stoned or what?"
The look in Gary's eyes strayed from terror
to something that should have warned us to
leave, but instead we decided to hang
around. "Come on man. Get up," I said. "We
need a fucking beer and some pancakes." Gary
not only struggled to get himself off the
floor, but also looked just about as pissed
as I had ever seen him. "You fuckin' snide,
shit eating pukes." He screamed at the top
of his lungs, lunging at us with his fists
in the air, ready to fight. I not only
didn't want to fight Gary, but I had no
desire to go to the floor with a fat man in
his underpants.

"You want to fight us with shit stained
looms?" my brother shouted, throwing his
fists up ready to return fire once Gary made
a move. "You cracker jack shit eating fuck,"
Gary screamed, jumping around like some
hairy ass ape trained to guard the back door
for three bananas day. "If the fuckin' cops
get called, I'll do life."

It was typical for Gary to yell random
obscenities at me, threatening my life the
next time I beat down his door. I did it
often, but I could usually shut him up by
making a comment about the jack off stains
on the front of his underwear. "Do you wear
the same drawers everyday, or are you really
pettin' the ol' walrus for Jesus that damn
much?" I would say to him. Guys like Gary
Fullerton will go to their graves without
ever admitting to something as ordinary as

jacking off. He would say, "Hell no, I don't
need to do that. I've got women who do it
for me." It didn't matter what you said, if
you boldly confessed to spanking your meat
three to four times a day, Gary would always
deny, deny, deny. I would call him out by
saying "Goddamnit Gary, you're a fucking
liar… every man whacks his sack."
"Uhhnt-uh boy," he'd reply, blathering and
stuttering like a sixth grader being teased
in the lunch line. "I ain't no faggot son."
"A faggot?" I'd say, "Listen dick ass,
punchin the munchkin doesn't make you a
faggot. Maybe thumb fuckin your own asshole,
but definitely not jerkin. And you know what
jackass? Sometimes it's just necessary, and
you can eat my balls because your crusty ass
looms are the same color as mine… yellow."
That was generally Gary's cue to throw a
cold beer on the bar, and head upstairs to
put on some pants.

My brother didn't hang around Gary's as much
and truth be told, the two of them didn't
really like each other. "You don't want none
of this shit stain," my brother yelled
watching him closely while Gary ravaged on,
bouncing around the back room, swinging
haymakers at absolutely nothing at all. The
chaos was edging my brother closer to going
in for the kill. I made every attempt to
calm them down, but then I got thrown off
for a minute because I spotted a collection
of retard crayon art hanging on the wall.
"What the fuck?" I thought to myself before
reading a portion of text written inside a
picture of a baseball playing cowboy riding

a unicycle. It said, "the unhinged memoirs of a sick dog, sponsored by the Special Olympics." I thought that sounded about right.

MICA'S MAD WHALE

There's a muffled old radio announcer who
has already given me the setting of my
story… two faceless people having a
conversation within the corridors of a cheap
hotel; a man, a women, a whore… The story
that they are telling me conveys emotional
distress, fear with some of the most
beautiful music, a sad ambiance with static
eyes and tears with the overtones of a
sitcom.

Animal lust. Nothing less for this 1950's
portrait of the American family… it's all
the same in black and white - a couch, a
lamp, a mother standing above her irony…
bored. There have been some questions asked,
but even fewer answers… Inside this home of
ours there are no details, everything is
vague. It is the secrets, the laugh tracks,
the paranoia - all of us well dressed
animals. There is one in particular; he
wears his wall street doom on the sleeves of
a corpse suit. He seeks the mansion, and
above all he is on an illusion quest for
opportunity.

From my window, I watch disoriented women
sidewalk nature as they seek an entrance to
share the trance with one of their own…
These people have no idea what to expect,

yet they are expecting something. In this world the butler isn't black, but the coffee always is. Tea time is served over the prophecies of décor and murder. The conversations are polite when carried on by actors who easily confuse these tales of ghosts and never happen endings.

Evil is the small boy who died just before his conception. The "half born" has the market over all of the stillborn pasts that have yet to happen. To never know when and where the time will come when you will turn around to find you simply never existed. We are these people. We stand across the room from ourselves. Now the prophecy has come true. A man in the corpse suit watches Hollywood from the top of the stairs… The genesis; the Eve's drop.

The story has not yet been written, but the film is complete. All of these characters are answering to a jewel thief, a wicked witch playing "harps of sex,"… blowing kisses. Blue is too dark for this set because it has a way of overshadowing the looking glass. Headaches and silence; WE BEGIN AT 35. Apologies for truths that could never be lies… "I'm sorry for you. I don't feel sorry, but I am SO sorry." Now the blue is far too dark for this man to look for the actual color of the set…

Through that door is the search for a disappearance of a man running from himself just to understand why the looking glass exists inside of such a blue set. It's a life that never existed, but what was inside

of that life was another country, with
another life that looks just like that whore
over there. There is a confession to some
very bad things to come, a reflection with
the wrong color of hair, but with the
absolute brilliance in blood. There is a
number, this color is the number from a
grave, a romance through the looking glass.
A black suit and no soul, sunshine is a
seven over my right shoulder; wag the tail
or gnash the teeth. They continue to borrow
their weight in something unknown, to feel
obligated to dissect a man and everything he
comes with… home now. I cannot hear one
single faggot who understands that I am not.

A sincere threat, bonded by the vows of the
animal before procreation, consequences, or
a pat on the back.
Alice is later than the infant who gives in
to its beverage just before the beginning of
the next scene. Romance is only dinner, the
rest is music… Sex ruins romance and
conversation, and cheapens a really
goddamned good drink. As the food is served,
it comes as quite a surprise that no one
will partake in the feast. The appetites of
these monsters can only be found at the
bottom of a bottle of black holes where each
one of our exact weights carry us straight
to the bottom. Dinner is romance. Italian
food is nice as soon as the bread comes. The
Italian feast is symphonic for sex; it is
the symphony that ruins the beautiful music…
It is the illusion of love that cheapens the
whore. The set is still too blue.
For each of these characters, real life,
without them knowing it, is now the past; a

story that never existed. It was never told, but from death they find everything that they ever wanted at the shallow end of the bottom, the orgasm inside the blue. Romance is dinner… You are being watched. The prophecy has not yet come true.

Why am I remembering another life when I can't even remember who I really am? I have become one or more characters in this script, if it does in fact exist. It is likely that I have only become an extra in the script that was never written. I am not aware of this. I only know because I have no idea. Something tells me that it was the girl all along…

Now the set is red, but for those chasing it, nothing has changed. The blue is bright white. The man cannot see inside the dimension in which he dwells. A spirit through a dirty window vanishes, but to where? Perhaps without a trace it has crossed over where sound cannot see enough of the pitch to understand that a plot for this goddamned story is not needed. A script is cheap. A wall is an illusion, and a lamp cannot be shut off in a film that has not yet been conceptualized. I watch as the woman dances with her animal on the red set.

It is apparent that she has lived among the whores — sex, slaves, love covers her eyes from the static. She can now taste these streets where the pussy has become a radio show produced in mono and broadcast over the saddest frequency. The show is always subject to change and brought to you by you

or her or him. It is true that the message
is not audible, yet it is understood. She is
him dressed as them behind a wall. All they
really want is the girl; to open the door
and fall into a tiny crack in this goddamned
town… The only way to hell.

The first breakfast in hell takes place on a
devil stained carpet under shades of 70's
lighting… All of us eat with strangers as
the violins play against the ticking of a
very expensive clock. Breakfast is romance
for the blind… You sir have insulted me and
ruined my new suit. I'd rather fuck you and
die again inside of these flames than be
burned at the stake simply because no one
could understand that all I wanted to do is
fuck… Now fuck me.

This is the saddest story that can never be
written… All of you animals can play with
your candles, but this apartment is now
vacant. None of you know the shadows, but
most would agree that we've not only been
here before, but we've been here for a long
time. This place in which we now dwell is on
the other side of hell. We are the faces
with no souls who once told the tales of
faceless men. Our oldest stories are worn on
the sleeves of the looking glass… We have
been here for a long time, something that
happened before the script was ever thought
of and goddamnit to hell, it is something
that will out die, just as much as it will
out live every last breathe of this fucking
universe.

At this very moment, it is she who dances on the red set that we shall call Alice. The girl is heavily sown under the doom of the November sky - the sky that has somehow found its way past the songs of September. All of the others have diarrhea by now, their pussies hurt, and the cum is gone. Rapists and pedophiles come out after this. They sing to their reflections in the mirror while the whores eat each other out on Broadway.

The scene will end choreographed as if it were a high school musical, but the paintings they leave behind are nothing but flannel and violence. Some may ask, "What is love?" while those of us who know, know that love was simply dinner… nothing more.

Upstate New York is a special kind of hell. It's the one that lives inside of the closet of a starving artist convention. Now we must kill the second coming as if it were a rotten slice of bologna on stale rye bread. All of the coven's children will dance in these circles before the seven digits can be dialed. The girl loves the tone of the animal, but cannot understand what it is that he is trying to tell her over the subliminal messages. The day before last, the girl told me about the time I killed her with a tire iron. She said she wasn't angry about it anymore, and that after it happened, she lived just long enough to manipulate her soul into becoming just like her… She was now alone.

Dreams are our realities without actually having to see them to know they exist. Agree to consider considering your light and reflections as familiar. My god, you can't just lay there bleeding to fucking death just because you feel like the devil in a pair of pajama pants. Down here, it is wise to carry a fucking knife when you stab somebody in the dark.

A long haul is our journey. The year is unknown. The time of death is today but just not right now, yet depending on the year in which everything unwritten is published, all of this might be something from the past. You'll see. Goddamnit you will see that I am a monster, a chariot for the corpses, who has a saw like sweet tooth used for nothing else but to devour. This story was not in the papers, but I have seen the headlines: The animal lives, unsuspected cruise ship bbq is happening yet it will not sink… The dirt is too dry to kill or to have dinner.

The circus midget will attempt to sell you a little more life dressed up in some quasi-political humor and disappear without a goddamned trace before you are able to determine which he actually was - small or political. You will never know the type of man who drowns the clowns while paying all of the others to stay very fucking far away…
"Show me how to fuck like you."
"First, turn off the light and take this medicine."
"I'm spinning…where is it that I have gone to?"
"This is my home. It will be yours someday."

"How do you know this?"
"Because, I have the fucking keys."

I AM THE PROPHECY… YOU ARE THE PAST.

I saw it in her eyes, through her eyes, and
when she had finally seen enough, I had
become her, standing inside of something
intimate and vile… The year is still
unknown.

Mike Adams

THE APACHE MOTEL
5535 N. Lincoln Ave – Chicago, Illinois 60625

12 April 2008

THE APACHE MOTEL: CHICAGO, ILLINOIS

I can feel Siberia in heat; a cold ghost, a charred
army of dying spider clones crawling on the back of
my neck. The streets of America reek of murder lust,
the stench of a dead vagina rat. My witness is; this
land once dwelled by oblivious society has become a
graveyard of dumpster sleepers, cannibalism and
suicide missions... one thousand times around a
crooked spine.

From within these four walls, room 111, I can hear
the drip, drip, dripping of an old whore's rusty
pipe in the east and the faggot clutches of prison
tits in the west. The butcher's ooze surrounds me,
seeping from these warts and boils festering around
my elastic pucker hole. It is time to pull the kills
witch guys... So, swing that axe Jack. Will the
recessive thematic be castration or circumcision?

What did we expect to find? Chicago is devastating
and torrential; it is all laid inside the mud pew of
this midwestern death row October, everything seen
through the black and white desert Eye of Horus. The
city is at its full loom, hopelessly helpless to a
grim legion of Devilitist. It's a goddamning hollow
thunder ground out there; Ann & Archie's Circus of
Serpents are hissing and spiting from the deepening
bowels of Parasite Alley. Their guts swell and bloat

from partaking in the tainted Puddles of the
Pheocies. The wrenching of the amoebas have eaten
them alive, belly and fucking brain.
These reports, should you choose to enlighten the
new world, shall exist as The Goddamned Chronicles
of Shred, the first and perhaps last chapter in
Whirled Pisstory, the latest Revolt in the Black
Death Scapegoat.

So it seems the real illuminate of the scripture was
lost in the pitch and slurs of translation. The
second coming is not, nor has it every been a
metaphor, nor a prophecy of the rapture, but through
alllllll of theeeeeeese eyes it has been made
clear that the goddamning ALL has risen and is
coming for each one of us. Those who have committed
their faith to the Quran and the Holy Bible must now
know there wasn't enough fact lain in between all of
those words, lines, and diseases of the Hebrew
textbooks to wage a Holy War. WE must have known all
of this was coming?

*"The enemy so much to be feared to retire
into Thrace, Leaving cries, howls, and
pillage desolated: To leave noise on sea and
land, religion murdered, Jovial Ones put on
the road, every sect to become angry."* —
M.N.

I finally met with the Irish priestess, Lizzie
McNeil… THE LAST LADY. She begged me to eat her out
in front of a crowded dumpster as some sacred rite
just minutes before the shadows of the abandonment
began slicing the Rosy Cross into the side of her
throat, banishing her goddamned soul to Hell,
although I am not convinced that we are not already
dwelling deep inside of an undiscovered gate. I
cannot see any numbers or equations or for that

matter, anything that resembles an exit. The Magdalena Alley of the Rising Clit Cult is plastered with desperation, crimson sigils, flag ash, religion is all a blaze, sub-assemblies of nigger thrill cults... all standing in line to be devoured by the greatest of famine.

The purest of Evil has taken the thrown dressed in cloaks of the Black Order, wielding fire from the serpent's staff. These infections, the so called Devilitists are nothing more than the most desperate of measures disguised as the golden hangman, circled, shaded, grudge fucked, crossed out, spelled backwards, and recited 149 times before this wrath child is dethroned and beheaded to be buried without a prostate underneath the center of Eden's regime... again and a-fucking-gain we must kill. Yet, this desperation is convincing and the abandon is obviously out of its mind.

Nevertheless, how can we blame them? We have all eaten the rotten seed from the wrong tree. The coil has been undone and venomous is its fangs. Nothing begins. So where does this all end?

We cannot petition you Lord with prayer! We must leave the Column of Raphe to burn... allow this world to reconstruct itself and live again, but only after all have died. For this is the only way. The bloody sickle nooses from my neck here in this chapel of the 111, but appears powerless. The reaping of humanity must finally come to rest on the Sabbath.

This I fear is the closing entry, left behind as a blueprint for the new world erection; to show all of those blinded by ignorance, the literal and those who surface without question that organized Faithist are hereby products of history and the chemistry of revulsion. The greatest plague has emerged without science and thus surpassed all scientists. The beast has resurrected, breast to backs, demons spreading seed; a plague that will not take the powers of ten before enlightenment or demise.

From God I can take no more... For no tunnel exists a light, only light through the peripheral soul. For God I can do no more... Here to paradise we go, brighter made is their woe, As Above, So Below...

Mike Adams

LOUDER THAN HELL

"Angel from below . . . I WISH TO SELL MY SOUL . . .
DEVIL TAKE MY SOUL with diamonds you repay I
don't care for heaven so don't you look for me to cry
AND I WILL BURN IN HELL from the day I die."
— Diamond Head

Traveling with a perverse combination of religion, ego, and a backhand of poverty across the face with a shotgun nigger dash of gay pride is the only way to travel across the country. It is likely the common man will not understand this. Few could. I have always known that such cander was possible, yet had I not seen it for myself, I would have always carried around some estute revelation of doubt. Unfortunately, this story is not one of fiction, even though the publisher of this work is sure to market it as such. This story is indeed based on factual accounts, and in no way are they or could they have ever been fabricated... Only those who ride winged creatures and whip daringly into the night with headless beasts tucked under their arms, those so disgusting that the naked eye cannot even begin to see them... It is only those who are pivoted on hell fire that are gifted enough to see this tale for what it really is. This demoralization is something that is created in time.... The sector is different although the remnants of shit all smell very much like the same asshole. We cross paths never questioning why we have been chosen to take part in someone's life or experiences within it.

66

Perhaps we are set there to make that experience more pleasurable, but it seems more likely that we are there to destroy it. Either way it is a golden goose covered in novelty and puke, and that makes me grin every time I am introduced to someone new. Nice to meet you?

To make the deepest cut in the world of music, an industry of scum humping coke fiends, those who make their livings out of sucking people like us dry, leaving us for dead whenever it becomes necessary, you must first understand just how dangerous these people really are. These people understand the work of the devil even if not traditional followers. They're fucking hypocrites and they will bury you if you are not the first to dig the grave...

St. Louis, Missouri
The Interstate Through Misery Leads to a Porn Mall with a Bible Belt

It was just the four of us. Although unique in orientation, culture, and God we had a lot in common. All of us loved music; we each had two legs, and we were all fucking nuts - in the literal sense, as if there were any other. I was certain that this ride was going to be long. Perhaps it would never end. It was just as likely that I would be forever stuck in some rancid purgatory disguised as a mini-van for the godamning of all eternity. That was unless we actually reached Los Angeles, a destination that for me was just as fablous as the existence of heaven and hell. If such a city did in fact exist, it would be there that I would lose touch with those who are human, shaking hands while looking over my shoulder, never knowing what sort of rat would attemt to eat me up and shit me out. Vermin will eat the very last crumb of anything with an odor, and I had no doubt that our souls would soon be laying face down in the garbage just waiting for something to take a bite out of the center of our assholes.

It is for this reason that I never wiped my ass. If someone is going to bite it then you had better be goddamned sure they are going to taste it. To leave an aftertaste in the mouths of beautiful people is something that gives me pleasure. To watch the rich and sculpted vomit themselves inside out was like whacking off day in and day out without ever showering, and then allowing some bruised blonde to give you alley head outside of some bar. Putting disgusting things in people's mouths is the only thing that has ever made me sincerely smile - that keeps me smiling. In fact, if you ever enter a room and I am there, just drinking and smiling, I caution you not to kiss anyone.

It was somewhere around St. Louis, just about two hours from home, when I started to eat the pills. God, if I can just wake up in Vegas long enough to hit it big on the nickel slots then I can walk away from this torture and start all over - wash my dick; try to live right. Unfortunately a light sleeper is all the same under the influence, and the rambling and barking of people who you call friends, in high enough doses, is enough to make a person want to throw themselves out of a moving vehicle and onto their head. Yet, two hours into a trip across country was not nearly close enough to the riot point. Not even half-way would be sufficient; If I started swinging punches now I would probably find myself stranded in a Missouri wheat field grazing for dinner or worse, forced into taking a job working the cash register at one of the many off highway porn shops. I guess that wouldn't be so bad - Minimum wage, a tip jar; I bet I could make a small fortune just sucking off nigger truckers in the back lot. I never have sucked a dick, but I have witnessed it – and it is for that reason I am certain that it wouldn't be for me. I had better scheme up a new plan. Surely these people, my friends, are going to prove to be better company than straight niggers bartering with cash and nick knacks for blowjobs. "It gets lonely out here bro!"

KANSAS
Freebird Fear Across the Misery State Line

The back wheels of the van hadn't even crossed the state line into Kansas before Toby Shain began running his mouth about a potential last minute booking in Salina behind a Long John Silvers.

"I think I can get us a gig on our way through Kansas" Toby said. "It would be good last minute practice before we get to L.A."

"Well", Briscoe replied, his voice producing a spoon full of dread. "Do you need to make a phone call or what?"

"The exit is just off the interstate," Toby said. "We'll just drive in and stop by the bar."

"What's this place called?" Briscoe asked, his dread now transformed into dismay.

"Chuckleheads!", Toby shouted.

"What kind of place is it?"

"It's a typical small town bar", Toby replied, laughing at Briscoe's pretentious prejudice towards the middle class blue collar culture.

"Are we going to have to play Freebird?" Briscoe spouted off in laughter.

"It sounds cool to me." I said. "See if you can get us free drinks."

"Gas money will do!" Briscoe said glaring back at me as if I was some three year old who had just kicked the back of his seat one to many times.

"True" I said. "But it has been a long day and I'm going to need something in order to play that bass tonight. I'm not playing in Kansas sober that's for sure - and why would any of us want to? This trip should be viewed as just that...a trip. The reality is that our experiences while together will have much more longevity than this band or the music we play...lets go for it all! Not to mention I may have swallowed too many sleeping pills!"

"Jesus Christ!" Briscoe shouted. "I'll buy you a couple of beers. It's good to see where your faith lies asshole. I just don't want you getting drunk."

"My faith lies in nothing!!!" I screamed. "Faith is for people with no common sense -and it's going to take more than a couple of beers before you have to be concerned for any state of drunkenness... When you see that I've pissed my pants then you can wade through the vomit."

"I'll just play for food," said Deni.

"Goddamnit girl," I shouted. "This place isn't going to have anything natural...they'll serve nothing but meat! Have you lost your mind!"

"We'll get some dinner," Briscoe scoffed. "We don't even know if they are going to let us play. Are you sure you don't need to call them first?"

"No" Toby said. "The exit is right in line with where we need to go."

SALINA, KANSAS
The Great Pentecostal War Nerve

We took exit two fifty-two towards Salina. It was apparent that the little town wasn't going to have much to offer. There was a part of me that was a bit nervous with the thought of taking this particular band to the stage here smack dab in the armpit of Lady America. If this bar was like any of the ones back home the locals were going to be looking for a couple of things from their entertainment. The guys were going to want to hear familiarity, something classic and depending on what they were drinking, something just a little bit twangy. For once, the women would be easier to please. We simply had to provide them with a strong beat... something they could shake their fat assess to; that was unless this bar was just a total disaster of the soul, a dark place where every patron sits mumified at the bar, drinking themselves into oblivion, pouring more and more misery onto their sagging tits and enormous beer guts well into the long hours of the night. Either way was fine with me. I didn't care. Selfishly the only thing I cared about was drinking beer, eating bacon cheeseburgers, and perhaps rolling my cock around in some whores mouth for thirty seconds or more. In a town shaped like this, a man shouldn't venture out into it with very high expectations, but it is a man's responsibility to reach out and take everything he can possibly handle. There is no such thing as standards and morals in a place like this. You were either going to eat

73

or be devoured. Whatever was left on your plate by the
time you rolled out after the lights went down was
entirely up to the strength of your gag reflex and your
rotten stomach.

"We should change the name of the band for tonight's
show," I suggested as we crossed a set of railroad tracks
on a deserted road leading into town.
"To what?" Briscoe asked.
"I don't know man." I said, not thinking I would even
get past the idea...I had no suggestions.
"How about Crackerjack Tattoo?" shouted Toby as if he
had been keeping the name firmly tucked in between
his pseudo-artsy self and the part of him that still very
much lived and died by the mullet.
"I fuckin' love it!" I yelled. "Lets go with it!"
"I think we'll just stick with what we have," Briscoe
announced from his dashboard podium.
"Whatever you want to do bro," I said, shaking my head.
"These hillbillies will eat us alive! We don't need that
type of press this early into the tour."
I was trying to use some subtle psychology on Briscoe
in order to get him to switch sides and perform under
the masquerade that Toby had suggested. Honestly, my
intentions were pure evil, but apparently I was the only
one aware of it. Once I stepped out of the van and into
some strange small town bar, my Mr. Hyde would rear
its demon and begin to lay to waste much of everyone
who dared to come into contact with me.

It wasn't that I was some sort of egomaniacal prima donna who expected anything and everything that he asked for as if I were this huge fucking rock star that made demands and stomped his feet until he got them. No, it wasn't like that at all. In fact, it was the opposite. I hated being a musician. Not so much actually being a musician, but I hated the stereotypes that went along with it. I hated the fact that too many years of bullshit bands and musicians had come and gone, leaving the aftertaste of something a bit worse than the whisky-shits in the mouths of any and all that had to deal with these miserable hacks on a daily basis. I simply hated them! I hated all of the phony camaraderie and the two faced handshakes. I hated all of the motherfuckers who couldn't have a conversation without talking about their new equipment or how we should get together sometime and "jam". I hated it! So for that very reason I allowed myself to come off the hinges while touring.

I firmly believe that once you leave your nest in the country to travel from the country performing music, swallowing swords, jerking off goats, or anything else that frames you and puts you on display, that you become, in a lot of ways, untouchable. You become a moving target and rarely are you in the same spot long enough to get caught. You have just enough time to wreak havoc on the town, it's bars, the women, and their families. You can lie, cheat, steal, rape, and possibly even murder; it all depends on how far you feel you can take it. For each city you perform and push the boundaries, the more balls and guts are worn on your

sleeve at all times. Whatever you choose to destroy is
all yours and those pathetic, fat, filthy pigs will not
have enough time to even take notice, much less build a
case. There was absolutely nothing to lose. In my time, I
had lost almost everything that most people try to hang
on to with both hands and feet. The thought of trying to
get it all back exhausted me to the point of actually
considering prison versus another failed try.

We drove around the streets of Salina for thirty minutes
or more waiting patiently for Toby to locate a bar that
he confessed he had not seen in over fifteen years.
Briscoe was taking odds that the bar was probably
closed or burnt to the ground for insurance money, but
in a small town, a hometown bar is a detrimental
fixture within the community. Close its doors and you
have just cut off all honest after hours camaraderie as
well as put a tourniquet around the remainder of the
dirty sex men choose to have with their wives and farm
animals. There was no way a bar in a town this size
would ever close. Even if the owner wanted out
desperately and ran out of town punching preachers,
pissing on tombstones, and butt-fucking basset hounds
he would still be expected to carry on business as usual
come nine o' clock the next morning.

Toby finally located the bar after spotting an old
Penecostal church where he told us he had screwed his
wife years ago while in town visiting her parents. Just
the thought of Pentecostal sex made me cringe; I didn't
want to hear too much for fear that it might cause some

rare psychosamatic blockage that would hinder my ability to get a really stiff erection - possibly for the rest of my life. To this day, I cannot pass a Pentecostal property without the illest of thoughts... Thoughts of heavy breathing forced from mouths attached to wild, unskilled boners, and extremely hairy bush.

"I'm going to go in here and talk to someone about getting us a show tonight," Toby said, while parking the van. "How much money should I ask for if it comes up?"
"I'm not worried about the money," Briscoe said, "but enough for gas would be nice though."

I knew at this point there was no sense in even starting up again. For some sick reason, Briscoe didn't feel like putting a price tag or any value at all on what we did. I didn't believe in that. In my mind, minus the obvious degeneracy, we were a somewhat interesting band. Interesting enough to denounce everything from junkies to liars yet employ them all. We were all hypocrites by the end of the day, yet some of us were fun to watch, and better than a lot of the dried crap that the media gets in bed with. So why be afraid to present a list of demands? Everything is a negotiation anyway; you start with everything and dwindle it down to something that everyone can live with. Just because we were asking for a gig from the parking lot like beggars, was no reason to cower. It was part of our well being Goddamnit! I didn't press the issue about the free booze, because I knew that if the bar agreed to let us play, more than likely

they would throw a few drinks into the mix. I was
counting on it. I figured I'd let Briscoe and Toby Shane
work out their skanky deal. Then I'd make some
amendments to it as I moved along... untouchable
remember?

After about twenty minutes, the van began to chill as if
we were being iced down for a cheap hooker in some
off highway trucker motel. Toby came out of the bar
with a smile on his face like he had just gotten to feel
some strange womans breasts, and gave us the thumbs
up as he crossed the street. When he got back into the
van Briscoe frantically started in on him.
"So what's the deal?"
"They said we could play tonight as the headliner." Toby
replied. "We got lucky, because they have original music
on Sunday nights."
"That's cool," Briscoe said. "I'm not to crazy about
headlining though."
"I'm not either!" I shouted. "We'll be playing for
ourselves!"
"Well, maybe we can work something out with them
once we get in there," Toby said.
"What about Deni!" Briscoe yelled.
"She'll just go on before or after us," Toby said, doing
his best to fake like he knew what the fuck he was
talking about.
"I don't care when I play," Deni replied.
"Are we going to get anything for this?" asked Briscoe -
suddenly concerned about the purse.
"Yeah," replied Toby.

Toby gave us the rundown of the deal for the evening: The bar was going to give us a three way split on the cover charge. We would also be given all of the free draught beer they had on special. This downed the others, but excited me. I lived my drunken life back home with mystery booze and I'll be damned if I would allow them to use it as a negative term in this deal. It excited me! But if we wanted anything in a bottle or mixed drinks we would have to pay full price. We were also given a ten-dollar food allowance, which is always plenty when you're ordering bar food.

"They want us to keep the food deal under our hats," Toby told us. "The local bands aren't getting any of that."

"Ha-ha-ha! We're big time baby," Briscoe screamed.

"Yeah, we are!" I wailed, swinging a high five towards Briscoe and missing the target. It was funny. In just a matter of hours the sleeping pills had eaten a hole the size of a quarter right in the center of my skull. At this point, I was a fucking retard!

"Load in isn't until six thirty," Toby instructed. "The manager told us to come back then and we could go ahead and get set up."

"Ok, its five now," Briscoe said. "What are we going to do for the next hour and a half?"

"Can we not just go in there and grab some beers?" I asked.

"No." said Toby. "They're not even open right now."

"Well is there any place we can go and grab a drink?" asked Briscoe.

Minutes later the four of us, looking as if we had just been dusted off of the crotch of some homosexual iron worker, walked into a little dive just a few blocks away from Chuckleheads. There were a couple of guys setting at the bar with flames shooting out of their eye sockets. These were the true lifers of Salina. They nearly caught our clothes on fire glaring at us as we walked through the door. You could see the confusion protruding from the bottom of their glasses as they thought about who we might have been. Silence filled the room and it was thick. As I glared back at the two bar stool samples, there was a part of me that wanted to turn things upside down - Rush up and grab one of them by their smelly shirt and tear them off the barstool with boner vengeance. Then after beating the lousy slob within an inch of his miserable life, spew something about how Uncle Geano wasn't just going to stand around while some piece of shit drank his pathetic life away before paying him what he owed. Then I would add that I was sent to either collect... or fuck him in the ass with the very bottle he was drinking from! This would surely disrupt the conversation even more, and probably cause his buddy to haul ass out of the bar never to return again. The look in the mans eyes would turn to horror as he made a run for it... and right before the bastard got to the door I would scream "I love fucking dead beats in the ass!" "Come back and get you some!" He would never be heard from again.

Of course it was entirely too early in the day to be jumping on top of strange people and causing friction

between everyone in the band and in the room. These
guys and gals did not appreciate the beauty of a random
violent moment. So I just nodded my head at the two
gentlemen and proceeded to a table just to the right of
the bar. A surprisingly beautiful waitress greeted us.
"What can I get you fellas?"
"Do you have Guinness?" Briscoe asked while looking
around the room for any signs to answer his question
before she did.
"We have Heineken," replied the waitress. "That's about
the extent of our, you know, foreign beers."
"I'll have one of those," Briscoe replied.
"I'll have a water," said Deni.
Toby and I ordered Buweisers.
"Ya'll gonna be needing any menus today?"
"I think we're just going to have the drinks," Briscoe
told her.

The waitress smiled as she walked away from the table.
I smiled back and delivered her a wink that somehow
turned into a very heavy blink - not just with one, but
with both eyes. There is something about taking
sleeping pills and not getting any sleep; It makes you
feel like you're deep inside a poorly drawn cartoon.
Now I was beginning to feel as if everyone around me
believed that I had just been released from the state
hospital. Blinking heavily was a sure sign of psychosis, a
twisted mind naturally trying to find a way out. It was
far too early for that beast to start rattling his own
cage. Once the teeth are shown the only obvious
protocol is to bite down. It is from my past experience

that I know this; you've got to ease into it. The only problem was you could never tell if the rattle was real or a fluke.

There was definitely something set into motion upon our arrival in this bizarre land; I could feel it. This life of miles and strangers on top of bullshit and loss was not for everyone and most certainly not for anything or any person weaker than the ghosts that float between the souls of all who have been here before us. It is certain death for most that live this way, and only those with some really strong illusions of luck or the strength to perservere past the idiocy of it all will survive. The trick is finding strength before losing too much of yourself and the people who surround you. Each town, city, or highway seen once has been seen time after time, even if not the same place at all. As the years pass we find ourselves staring out of the window a different way, and every time it rains we touch the glass with the memory of the day at the end of our fingertips.

I always missed the things that I took for granted while on the road. In ways it made me honest with myself. Rather than giving into the lust of escapting it, there was no better way to infiltrate the psyche and siphon your feelings than being seperated from those you truly needed and wanted within the big picture. The predicament occurs once the outline was drawn. Your position as artist quickly becomes one of the subject, and the texture and subtle touches were never put in to place. As years pass, your quest for the BIG picture becomes more and more cluttered by all of your failed attempts on the same canvas with fading silhouettes of everything you figured out once but forgot it one more time than that.

This life is not for the weak... or so I have heard. For those that it consumes, it makes everything beautiful and ugly; Each day brought to life with our hands over our face all end in laughter and love, no matter how minute. We are relentless beings with the souls of demons and the tears of children dwelling deep inside of our hearts. We live for this, godless and tired, hungry for more... Rock and Roll.

It was now time to go to work. We had come this far and no matter where our heads might have been just hours ago, somehow we found a way to collect ourselves. Our indiscretions were now firmly tucked into the front of our pants. I knew that in time and not much of it, that they would be pulled out again for all to see... Strangers would be astounded; friends would just shakes their heads. The performance would actually take place as soon as the amplifiers were unplugged and the booze started to flow, with no regard for how much money was coming out... or out of whose pockets.

At this point the show would go down in infamy and we would never be allowed back. The venue, perhaps even the state, would run us out of town and we would be lucky to escape with our balls still attached! Kansas was a bold place for a trial run, but a good show would not be enough. My thought was that if we could somehow burn the entire state to the ground before crossing the line into Colorado, then we would surely be doing something right. It would be our mark, a goddamned smoke signal to the dismal and oblivious of California. "We are on our way you sacks of sunshine and porpoise shit. Hose down all that you love!"

We arrived back at Chuckleheads for our load in at six-thirty sharp. There they were - the addicts, the scoundrels, and the faggots; those who called themselves artists and musicians, already gathering wallflower style, enthralled in their shameless prima donna promotions, local gossip and tech talk. I wanted nothing to do with it and vowed to kill or die trying in order to avoid it. This was it - a built in bullshit society that surrounded the supposed music scene. It was embarrassing and lazy. All of these people shared the same face, backed by the same lack of ambition; most of them with absolutely no guts at all. Poseurs like these can only show bravery in front of their mirrors, or family and friends two weekends a month. They are primped and glamoured blasphemy on a post it note stuffed inside the most microscopic crack of what dirt was left behind by one of the many bottom feeding footnotes of bastard rock and roll. These people were scams.

The truly bitter and subjectively psychotic aspect of this group of louses would come right after I am forced to meet them and try not to come across as a giant hairy asshole while making every effort to acknowledge them in conversation. In venues like this, it was like being stuck inside of a conference center with no windows during some Rock God convention weekend - and everyone in the room was convinced that somehow real life consisted of this. Where were these people at really? These parasites had stolen the identities of their idols and were now wearing them like royaly free snot smeared across their sleeves; the only thing making them different is some goddamned assumed name. These were the generic versions of madmen, which were far worse than the real thing... Extremely dangerous. I couldn't bare to be around leeches like this for long.

It sure made it a hell of a lot harder to pick the genuine out of a crowd simply because there weren't many of them. They were much harder to pick out of a line-up. It was funny, gruesome, annoying and extremely common. It was truly one of the most predictable environments... and I chose this as a career!

There is nothing glamorous about this pathetic scene. In this world, glamour comes through experience and the ability to aquire an honest perspective based upon that experince. Success, like cocks and tits, come in all sizes, but every success, no matter how small, comes with a price...

It is not this scene that I love; it is not the reason I continue to play music. The life of or the illusion of the life of Rock and Roll is for sadists and idiots who can only find acceptance from others before, during, and after 45 minute sets of stage time. Rock and Roll is my "Way of life." THERE ARE NO EXCEPTIONS! What seperates me from the sadistic idiot? As with anything, if you want it bad enough you must be prepared to do whatever it takes to make it happen. I believe the first step is to claim a spot on the ladder of legends and icons by eliminating the large percentage of supposed artists who, upon witnessing the magnitude of your abilities, will join the ranks of grocery store check out girls, fast food employees, roofers, and all the other remedial talent within their town...

I followed Briscoe into the saloon and took a seat at the bar while Briscoe stepped in a bit further to take a closer look at the layout of the stage and sound system. Toby and Deni filed in just a few moments later after stopping to bullshit with one of the degenerates loitering outside. Who knows what they wanted. I was just grateful that they didn't ask me for it.

"What can I gettcha?" asked the bartender throwing a wet towel over his shoulder placing both of his hands on the bar waiting for me to answer.
"I'm with one of the bands," I replied. "I'll have whatever is free."
The man smiled and shook his head.
"What band are you with son?"
"The Dicksville Conspiracy," I replied. "We're the ones from... Indiana."

"Maggie!" the bartender yelled across the room to a redheaded woman who was changing a light bulb above one of the pool tables.

"Does the... ahhh, Dicksville Conspiracy get free drinks?" he asked doing his best to articulate the name of our band.

"Who?" she asked.

"The Dicksville Conspiracy...from ahhh, Indi-ana?" he replied in a way that sounded as if he questioned the existence of such a state.

"O' yeah those boys from out of town," she replied. "They get the draft special hun. Everything else is regular price."

"Alright," he said, shaking his head like he understood. "I thought that's what we gave the bands, but I just wanted to make sure."

"That sounds good to me," I said. "I'll just go with whatever is free and alcoholic, but nothing alcohol free."

The bartender laughed as he poured me a mug of beer. I sat there looking around the bar, scanning the establishment for anything unique. Places like these were all the same. In fact, it reminded me off home. It was a sausage lodge at best, catering to construction workers and a handful of regulars, jealous men who brought their wives along to keep them from fucking around on them while they sat up at the bar all night. They knew from experience that their old ladies wouldn't sit around the house all alone for long before screwing someone else. For men like this, coming home

drunk and listening to some nagging had nothing on
walking through the door and finding another man
pissing on his tree, violently humping his old lady, and
eating up all the goddamn food.

Very much like the bars back home, this one too had
random signs full of pure Midwestern wisdom pasted all
over the walls which, unlike the bars back home, were
built out of old railroad ties. Most of the bar room
philosophy was put in place for laughs - Others to
caution your behavior.

Rule #1: The bartender is always right.
*Rule #2: If the bartender is wrong, refer to rule number
one.*

Do not drop cigerette ends on floor
as they burn the hands and knees
of customers as they leave.

Notice:
If you're drinking to forget,
 please pay in advance.

The bartender sat a beer down in front of me and for
some reason decided to strike up a conversation.
"So what kind of music do you guys play?" he asked. I
could not count the number of times that some rebel
biker looking bartender, who surely had his coming of
age during the Vietnam war, bothered me with that
same annoying question. But he seemed like a nice

enough guy, so rather than say something that may come across as rude, I thought I'd make an attempt to hit him with something he had never been dealt before.

"I'm not sure." I replied. "I haven't heard any of it yet."
"Haven't heard it!" he shouted. "What do you mean?"
"I mean I haven't heard any of it."
"How can you play in the band if you haven't heard any of the music?"
"I never said I was in the band," I replied. "I just said I was with them."
The man just starred at me with a confused bitch slapped look hanging off of his furrowed face.
"Look, I was hitchhiking," I said. "I think it was somewhere just outside of St. Louis and these guys pull over and give me a ride." I could see his confusion transforming into genuine interest.
"A few miles up the road, they asked me if I would help them out."
"With the band?" he said, now back to confusion. "Can you even play an instrument?"
Just as I was ready to answer, he was summoned for a round of beers and a high-ball by some lady at the other end of the bar. After he was finished, he came back over and hit me with more questions.

"So you really don't know those guys?" he asked, trying to remember exactly where our previous conversation had ended or where the next should begin.
"Well, from what I can gather," I replied. Leaning in closer, as if to tip him off that what I was about to say

was a secret, "The grey haired guy over there is the leader, some sort of traveling pervert – a cult leader or something."

"A cult!" he shouted.

"Shhhhh..." I said, looking over my shoulder. "Don't say that shit too loud. The one with the mustache, the drummer... I'm pretty sure that dude's packing heat. I don't know what their intentions are but they can't be good."

"Man, are you pulling my leg?" the bartender asked, trying to get a last minute grip on reality.

"Why would I make this up? I think these fuckers are the real electric gypsy! Why else would they just show up on your front door asking for a gig?"

"So, no shit?" he said, turning his half ass smile into the type of face you might see a man give while poorly bluffing during a card game.

"No shit... Say, can I get another one of those beers?"

The bartender poured me another drink. I could tell that he was not only confused but somewhat oblivious to how this whole goddamned conversation started. Even I wasn't completely sure where it all came from. It just did, and for the first time all day I wasn't bored with everything around me. So I dug just a bit deeper into my relentless sack of bullshit and threw some more of it in his face.

"Listen," I said. "Did see that girl that walked in with us?"

"Yeah," he replied, setting another beer down in front of me.

"I think she is their sex slave or something." I said this with the pure intention of tossing him straight over the edge while his back was turned. "I've watched both of them touch her in places I don't feel right repeating, and honestly, she doesn't act like she likes it very much."

"Why haven't you tried to stop them?"

"Survival," I replied. "Motherfuckers like that are why the morning news was created. Personally, if I'm going to make the news, I want to be alive to see it," I told him as I took another swig from my mug. "Look, I had better go before they start getting suspicious." I said as I swiveled my seat to the right of the bar.

"Suspicious?" the bartender asked.

"Keep those beers coming chief." I said, maintaining the kind of eye contact that speaks trouble without having to say it. "It's going to be a long night."

I stepped off of the barstool and walked into the performance area with the others.

"You guys should introduce yourself to the bartender," I said. "That way he knows your face before he gets too busy. Hell of a nice guy."

"We need to get the equipment in here before we start drinking," Briscoe shouted. "Someone forgot to tell the other bands that we were playing last and one of them already has their kit set up."

"Well, let's not headline this circus!" I shouted. "It's going to be the equivilent of a county fair talent show anyway. Just tell them everything is cool and that we prefer to go on as early as possible."

"I'll talk to them," Briscoe said. "Who's in charge? Do you know?"

"I think I'm going to grab a beer," Toby said. "I'll just explain to the bartender what happened and that we are fine with going on earlier."

"Get me another one while you're up there, will you?" I asked.

"How many have you had?" Briscoe shouted.

"This is my second," I replied, knowing damn good and well that it was my third.

"Plus the two you had down the street," Briscoe said throwing his hands into the air and setting them on top of his head.

"You can't count those," I replied, trying to defend myself from the inevitable lecture that was coming my way.

"Look, I don't want you playing drunk!" Briscoe shouted. "This tour is costing a lot of money, and I want to leave a good impression."

While Briscoe continued to banter on, I could see the bartender staring at me with some concern. Briscoe had a bad habit of animating himself when he was angry. From a distance, he looked like a cranked out televangelist damning to hell all that crossed his path. The bartender's imagination seemed to be running wild. I could tell he was nervous; He was beginning to look like a barn cat that had been raised on moldy Hamburger Helper and spoiled milk. I made eye contact with him and raised my hand to let him know that everything was all right. I had to let him know that this outburst wasn't the perversion he was waiting for. That would come later. From the look in his eyes, I could tell that he was just seconds away from jumping over the bar and bashing Briscoe in the back of the head with the billy club that he had tucked back there with him. I had seen that look many times before but never this early in the evening. The sun had not even gone down, and already the tremors of violence were rattling inside of at least one mans head. With something as putrid as this in the works, it was conceivable that this would be the first and last show of the tour.

I sat down next to Deni on a small bench along the wall that I recognized to be an old church pew. I always knew that somewhere out there someone would find a way to incorporate religion and booze without including overzealous Catholic rituals. Briscoe made his move and left to sit with Toby at the bar. They were watching, what appeared to be, a World War II documentary on a small television just above the bar. I watched Briscoe summon the bartender, waving his hand around as if being coy, yet becoming somewhat frantic seconds later. He ordered a drink and sat down next to Toby. The two of them sat at the bar more than likely discussing the documentary, or how tired they were from traveling all day. I could clearly see the bartender had taken it upon himself to get to the bottom of the story that I had fed him. I couldn't tell what they were talking about, but it must have had some subtle relevance to the animal I

helped conceive and torture minutes earlier. The
bartender began to look as if he had gone full blown
schitzophrenic, mumbling and shaking his head,
occasionally looking back at me for the kind of help
that I couldn't possibly give him.

"Why does the bartender keeping looking at us?" Deni
asked.
"I'm not sure," I replied. "He's probably just checking to
see if I need another drink."
"Probably," Deni said. "I think Toby forgot about you."
"Yeah. Actually, I believe Briscoe has it in for me this
round," I replied.
"He seems really high anxiety. Does he always get this
way before he plays?"
"Seems like it," I replied, knowing damn well that the
neurotic fever that had commited Brick Briscoe for life,
carried a weight far beyond that of simple anxiety. I
had witnessed it first hand, and I was absolutely
positive that I would see it again before this whole
sideshow and porn circus was said and done. It was just
a matter of time.

The beer was shooting straight through me. Even
though I tried to ignore the initial urge, I couldn't seem
to fight it. I could feel my bladder filling up as well as
the gnashing jolts of pain shot through my kidneys.
"This is it," I thought. "All of the years as a
promiscuous booze hound is about to kill me." I stood
up quickly, franticly running for the bar hoping the man

behind it would be able to act as liaison between me and a quiet place to spill it or die.

With what could have been mistaken as an ambush, I squeezed in between Briscoe and Toby Shane grabbing them both by the back of their shirts.

"I don't know what you guys did," I cried out in torture. "I think my goddamn kidneys are shutting down!"

They began laughing hysterically followed by some smart ass comment from Briscoe about having poisoned me with plans to donate my body to science.

"What?" the bartender screamed.

"Where's your restroom," I asked him painfully and in complete desperation.

The man seemed to have forgotten the layout of the place for a moment but then waved me in the general direction. "Back there. Back there to the right!" he shouted.

The shit box was small and repugnant with no way of locking the door. "The cleaning lady must have the day off," I thought to myself, holding my breath - wondering how long it would take before failing kidneys and lack of oxygen would lay me down in the remenants of every drunken male in Salina. The clamors from the other side mixed with the fear of an abrupt invasion of privacy was infecting me with stage fright.

"Goddamnit!" I shouted aloud cursing the unknown psychosis that had damned my inner animal, and made it almost impossible for me to effectively use a public toilet. I did my best to try to relax and soon it was all over. I could breathe.

As I stepped back into alcohoic society I was almost thrown off my feet by a thunderous roar coming down like the vicious hand of a god. I saw Toby and Briscoe being surrounded by three large, corn fed men who appeared to be waiting for the kill switch. The bartender was jumping up and down, pointing his finger erratically at Toby, and screaming at the top of his lungs. The outburst seemed to have stopped time. It looked as if everyone within close proximity to the riot was getting ready to be sucked into a dark hole and sent straight to hell. Nothing but silence was able to bind this bartender, who seemed to have slid right off of the edge of humility and on to a war nerve.

"You got a gun in here motherfucker!" The bartender shouted, still poking his finger across the bar into Toby's face.
"A gun?" Toby shouted. "I don't know what the hell you are talking about!"
"If you fuckers think you're going to come into my bar with a fuckin' gun, I've got some news for you sons of bitches!" The bartender screamed, continuing to yell with a raspy fury that would surely turn him into a mute by morning.

I had created a monster. The wrath that was richocheting off of every wall in the bar was about to hit someone – possibly even me. I desperatey wanted to try to diffuse the situation, but couldn't think of any way to do it without being beaten by both sides and thrown out the back door like a stray cat. It was lunacy - far too serious for any simple reprieve.

The bartender looked as if he was running out of things to scream about when the tide fell behind and the tsumnami rushed in.

"...and just what do you boys think you're doing with that girl back there?" the bartender, who I heard someone call Paul, asked.

"What girl?" Briscoe replied, looking as if he was ready to puke at any second.

"The one with you motherfuckers," Paul shouted back.

"Deni?" Toby cried out in question or maybe it was confusion.

The group of three that had surrounded Briscoe and Toby Shane, had now grown to about six or more. Now the locals were calling for action, shouting their battle cries into the crowd - "Kick his ass!"; "Yeah! Get em' Paul!" Briscoe and Toby Shane were doing everything they could to try to calm the bartender down and have him call off the heavy guard behind them. They were scared and restless, and everyone who had joined in was beginning to realize that it had come down to fight or flee. Some had that attractive option, while others were luck poor and locked into a chain linked fence of pure goddamned violence.

Just then, like a starving wild cat, Deni jumped in between the crowd of people that had Briscoe and Shane fully guarded with no way out. "Stop this! Stop this right now!" She screamed at the top of her lesbian lungs. "Leave these guys alone. Why are you doing this?" Everyone in the room seemed taken back by her frantic outburst. The bartender looked more dazed than ever. Almost teary eyed from all of the excitment. It was then that I really started to feel as if I had crossed the line. The situation, although restless and intense, was entertaining, and I had become starved for what was next to come. I had reached the point of forgetting the people involved were my friends and that I was the one who had caused this. Of course when I came to my senses, I realized that I had better cut my losses, and I snuck out the back door just past the bathroom and into a muddy alley.

I walked around to the front of the bar and sat down on the curb trying to think of how I was going to be able to walk along both lines of this story without getting my ass kicked by the bartender, his patrons, and my friends. There was absolutely no way I was going to get away with this now that Deni had stood up and cosigned for Briscoe and Toby Shane. I had really rubbed things in the wrong direction; It was now just me against them... all of them.

I could still hear the commotion from the curb outside the bar. All of a sudden the front door opened, and Deni came stomping out just about as pissed off as one person can get. She was screaming at the top of her lungs; the tone made the words incomprehensible. It was then that she spotted me on the curb. "Those idiots think Brick and Toby have been raping me!"

"What? Where did they get a fucked up thought like that?" I replied, as if I was surprised by what she had said.

"Who knows!" she screamed, glaring at the bar door as if waiting for someone to come out so she could devour them. "Inbred, drunken, facists have the ability to conjure up anything in their pathetic small minds!"

As I sat there contemplating whether or not to tell her that this twisted torture was due to boredom and brew, Briscoe and Toby Shane came flying out of the bar.

"Can you believe those people?" Briscoe shouted.

Toby was red in the face, yelling like an ogre, "She could be my daughter!" - and something else about being married, having children and being a christian.

"What the fuck is going on?" I shouted in between their hostility and bulging eye balls, trying to convince them, as well as myself, that I had no idea what was going on. Briscoe was pacing the sidewalk with his head down and talking to himself. "I thought we were going to be killed!" He said this over and over again, pondering just how close to death he may have come.

None of them had any idea that I had caused the whole flaming shithouse. They really believed that, for no reason at all the bartender just went on a crazy binge of street justice on a couple of guys he had profiled as armed rapists.

"So we're not playing the show?" I asked.

"Fuck no!" Briscoe shouted. "As a matter of fact, if they see us out here too long, we are going to end up in a fight."

"Those cock suckers still owe me dinner!" I yelled.

We got into the van and stopped off at the Long John Silvers across the street for something to eat. I had the fish and chips. No one said a word until we got back on the highway headed for Denver. About five hundred miles to go...

WaKeeney, Kansas
The Inconvenience Store Showdown

It was at a convenience store somewhere in the vicinity of WaKeeney when everything really started to come to pieces. It was late, and apparent that our time on the road was quickly coming to an end for the night. The ruckus in Salina had really shaken everyone. We needed time to unwind, have drinks, and collect ourselves before screaming down the highway, trapped inside of this mobile purgatory any longer.

The most attractive plan any of us could come up with was to buy a twelve pack of beer, and make a mad dash across Kansas while it iced down in the back. Then, once we pulled into Denver, we would duck into the first available rest stop and drink it all before going to sleep for the night. Denver would mark our half way point across the country. We could take it easy and brave the cold highway once more when the sun came up.

We entered the store looking like we had just been run out of Salina by the calvary. For all we knew there had been an all points bulletin put out by local authorities in order to seize us before crossing the state line. It was also possible that there were composite sketches of us being faxed to all fuel emporiums across the state... But we didn't care. We started to walk across the parking lot as if we were going in to either audit the place, or

set it on fire. From the look on Toby's face it appeared
that if anyone tried to pull any of the shit they pulled in
Salina he would opt to burn it down. Toby grabbed the
door and flung it open, walking in as Briscoe caught it
before it closed, allowing me and Deni to walk in before
him. I heard Toby ask the clerk something about where
the cold beer was located, and watched as she pointed
to the very back of the store. Toby walked like a man
on a misson of salvation or terror. I knew that I had
better take it easy on him for the rest of the trip. He
was likely to do something rash just trying to protect
himself, and get locked up for life. I watched Toby pull
out a twelve pack as I was on my way to the bathroon.
When I got out, I saw Briscoe and Toby standing at the
front while the cashier stared at them with an
extremely annoyed look on her face.

As I got closer, I could hear what the chaos was about.
Toby was yapping away about how it was illegal in
Kansas for convenience stores to sell beer with an
alcohol content over three point two percent. What in
the Hell of God was he talking about?

Insight: Low-Point Beer (3.2%)

Low-point beer, which is often called "three-two beer," is beer that
contains 3.2% alcohol by weight (equivalent to 4% ABV). The term
"low-point beer" is unique to the United States, where some states
limit the sale of beer, but beers of this type are available in countries
(such as Sweden & Finland) that tax or otherwise regulate beer
according to its alcohol content.

The states of Colorado, Kansas, Minnesota, Oklahoma, and Utah permit general establishments such as supermarket chains and convenience stores to sell only low-point beer. In these states, all alcoholic beverages containing more than 3.2% alcohol by weight (ABW) must be sold from state-licensed liquor stores. Oklahoma additionally requires that any beverage containing more than 3.2% ABW must be sold at normal room temperature.

Missouri also has a legal classification for low-point beer, which it calls "nonintoxicating beer." Unlike Colorado, Kansas, Minnesota, Oklahoma, and Utah, however, Missouri does not limit supermarket chains and convenience stores to selling only low-point beer. Instead, Missouri's alcohol laws permit grocery stores, drug stores, gas stations, and even "general merchandise stores" (a term that Missouri law does not define) to sell any alcoholic beverage; consequently, 3.2% beer is rarely sold in Missouri.

Briscoe just stood there listening, staring blankly into the milk cooler, while Toby jammered on about how this was probably the last place to buy beer and how all the liquor stores were closed. Briscoe maintained his entransive state of disappointment toward the milk cooler while Toby stared at him, waiting for the go ahead. The clerk was staring at both of them with her eyes rolled halfway into her eyelids. I was waiting patiently on the sidelines. It was a showdown. Who would blink first? Who would make a decision? Who would dare shuttle another couple hundred miles in search for booze that was five point five percent or higher. Nobody was blinking... not even the clerk. All of a sudden Toby turned around and handed the clerk a twenty. The showdown was officially over. The reality of Toby Shane's executive decision ravaged Briscoe as he let out a heavy sigh, and headed out the door into the parking lot and back to the van. I followed.

I jumped into the passenger seat waiting for everyone to come together. Deni was sitting on the back bumper with the hatch up eating something she called trail mix that looked like petrified vomit. Briscoe climbed into the drivers seat continuing his pathetic blank stare of monk like silence... I did the same. Toby and Deni loitered around the back hatch, icing down the beer and some water that Deni had purchased while I was in the bathroom.

"Three point two my ass!" Briscoe yelled at the steering column. I was the only other person in the van but he didn't appear to be talking to me. I too felt his relentless cries of disgust and anger. I harbored the same raw emotion for the situation. I never chose to eat tofu because I prefer to eat steak. I felt the same about beer. Wasn't it enough that they produced a light beer? Now we have to settle for lighter? It isn't right! Here we are in the true depths of Middle America and the very politics of it were taking away something that was very American. We deserved the right to get buzzed, but that was now in the hands of the local government. It was apparent that we had better haul ass out of town before they stripped us of other simple rights.

Toby and Deni got back into the van; all of us were ready to get out of a state that had not only left us for dead, but tried to get us sober. All of us silently vowed never to return as we began once more in a westbound

blaze on Interstate 70 with our focus being on the end
of the day once we got to Denver, Colorado.
No sooner than Briscoe got up to the speed limit, we
passed a sign - Denver 385 miles. The last miles of the
day were going to be the longest. I stuck my hand down
the front of my pants, and passively fondled myself
while staring out the window into the blackest night. At
least I could still touch myself. No one seemed to notice
and if they did, they didn't mind. If they did, they were
so taken back by it all that they opted to ignore me
rather than encourage it with controversy. After a few
miles of absolutely nothing on the radio, I turned to ask
Toby Shane where his CD's were. Both Toby and Deni
had nodded off.
"You guys sleeping?" I whispered. Neither one
responded. "Well, they're either fast asleep or ignoring
me." I said to Briscoe as he adjusted his seat back as if
trying to find some level of comfortability.
"They're asleep already?" He asked, rolling his eyes.
"Well I guess it's just you and me."
"Yep" I replied while rummaging through the glove
compartment for the missing CD collection. "Do you
know where Toby put his CD's?" I asked, now shuffling
through the sun visor.
"I think he said that he forgot to bring them." Briscoe
said. "I think that is what he said this morning before
we picked you up."
"Well fuck!" I said in distress as I agressively flipped
through the radio stations trying to find something
tolerable.

"I don't want to listen to anything he has anyway!"
Briscoe shouted. "All he has is eighties death metal and
electric blues. I hate that shit!"
"Well it beats what I'm finding on the radio." I replied
still flipping through the stations. "You have your choice
between static, a few country stations that won't quite
tune, and on the AM side some religious rants from the
same types of people who ran us out of Salina!"
"What was all of that about anyway?" Briscoe asked
holding his mouth slightly open and shaking his head.
"I don't know man." I replied. "All I know is when I
came out of the bathroom you guys were surrounded."
"That guy just went off the deep end for no reason. He
kept calling us pedeophiles and predators. I was
absolutely mortified." Briscoe shook his head.
"Maybe you said something to set him off." I replied.
"What were you guys talking about when it all started?"
"I can't even remember!" Briscoe shouted. "We were
cutting up with each other but nothing that should have
provoked anything like that. Hell we were in a bar! I've
said worse in church!"
Briscoe didn't have a clue that I had single handedly
tormented the Salina snake. Maybe they didn't say
anything to set him off into a frenzy. It was possible
that between the lines of the story that I told, and his
overactive imagination that he had painted a picture so
disgusting that he would have snapped regardless of
their topic of discussion. They could have been talking
about saving the lives of innocent kittens and somehow
that would have translated into sacrifice and cult
fucking. They didn't have a chance.

I must have dozed off at some point. I couldn't have been asleep for long. At least it didn't seem like it after being awaken to Briscoe shouting into my ear as if it were New Years Eve. "Ninety miles to Denver baby!" I got right up and began to look around. Toby Shane and Deni were still passed out in the back. I was covered in a thin layer of cold sweat, freezing my ass off, just minutes from hypothermia.

"Where the fuck are we?" I asked, reaching over to turn up the heat.

"We just passed the town of Limon." Briscoe replied. "We should be there in less than an hour." I knew that our journey was just about finished for the night. Soon we would be camped out in the Rockies, indulging in cold booze and brisk mountain air. There was also that slim chance that a percentage of Denver hookers deemed it more profitable to work the interstate rest areas rather than hustle in the streets. If this was true, then I had planned to take full advantage of the service once I arrived.

"I talked to a meteorologist early this morning." Briscoe said, trying to look past his side window and into the sky. "He told me there was a chance of some heavy snow in Denver. He told me that he would take the southern route." I too tried to look past my window and into the sky, but no matter how much I squinted, I couldn't see anything.

"That shit looks clear to me," I said, laughing and shrugging my shoulders.

"Fuck a weather man!" I shouted, laughing a little bit harder, getting more and more excited about the imminent canned booze and the prospect of a rocky mountain hooker. "Let's just get drunk and find some hookers!"

"I don't think we're going to get drunk on a twelve pack of that piss water they sold us in Kansas," Briscoe said, almost knocking himself back into the same pathetic stare he had back in WaKeeney. "And I don't know about there being hookers in rest areas. It's cold outside dude, but I guess if you can find one..."

There was so much excitement going on between the two of us. As more and more road signs appeared and passed, the miles that lay between us and our sanctuary were dropping like flies. The ninety turned into sixty, turned into forty-five. It wasn't long after it turned into fifteen that we passed a Denver City Limits sign. We had finally made it.

Denver, Colorado
The White Knuckle Rockies and The Tragedy Of Morgan O' Daniel

Briscoe looked over at me with a huge grin pasted all over his face. "We'll need to get to the other side of Denver before we start seeing any rest areas." He said this as if helping me understand his next move. "We shouldn't have any trouble with traffic at this hour." He was now fumbling with the radio. "We should be able to get a decent station here." While he fumbled with the radio, I began to explain in great detail the things I planned do to any rocky mountain hooker that not only had a strong enough stomach to see me naked, but to also allow me to improvise with a beer bottle and Toby's toothbrush.

I had barely finished my delirious tirade when I spotted a snowflake on our windshield. "Is it snowing?" I asked, looking out the passenger side window once more to gauge the activity.

"Looks like it's trying. Doesn't it?" Briscoe replied. "Probably just flurries." Within seconds the flurry of flakes had turned into hundreds, skipping the thousands, then raining down it the millions. I lost count of the flakes just as we lost our visibility. Less than zero. The sight was unlike anything I had ever seen. The sky had switched from black to white. Inches upon inches of snow fell at once as if someone had just thrown a huge blanket over the entire city. Briscoe now had both hands firmly planted on the wheel with his

back arched and his eyes just three inches from eleven
and twelve. "See if you can find something about the
weather on the radio," Briscoe shouted with hopes of
hearing some unfamiliar voice assure him that it would
be over soon. I couldn't find a station with any news
during my first pass, but as I neared the end of my
second I heard what sounded like the news.

*...an accident at the intersection of Westminster and
Broomfield claimed the life of a Lakewood man early
yesterday afternoon. According to witnesses, forty-six
year old Morgan O'Daniel was traveling north on
Westminster. O'Daniel ran a red light and was struck by
a truck traveling east on Broomfield. O'Daniel was
pronounced dead at the scene...Now for your local
weather. Cold and snowy tonight with a high of thirty-
three. Accumulation could reach up to fifteen inches in
some places. Some higher elevations could see anywhere
from fifteen to twenty-three inches by the time this
front passes.*

Briscoe quickly lifted his right hand off of the steering
wheel and shut the radio off. "Why'd you do that?" I
asked, "I thought we needed to hear the weather."
"I need to concentrate!" Briscoe was riding the brakes
as if it made a difference. Our speed had now slowed
from sixty mph to somewhere around ten to fifteen
mph. It was treacherous, and our travels at the last hour
had become a fucking war that none of us were
prepared to fight. Two of our soldiers were still sacked
out in the back, and it appeared that it was up to

Briscoe and me to carry us all to safety. So fight we did. We watched as eighteen wheeled monsters slid off the highway and flipped off of mountains. I wish I could have seen their faces, as it would have been the first time I saw the face of a man right before he died. What does that face look like? A man holding a CB radio in hands trying to make last minute contact with his employer before careening down a mountain to be crushed on impact. This would soon be us. Our wheels had stopped rolling and now were in a full skid down the mountain on what appeared to be the highway.

"I'm pulling into the next rest stop," Briscoe cried out in a panic.
"We'll be killed if you don't!" I replied. "Did you just see that fucking truck go over that cliff?"
"I can't see anything!" Briscoe shouted.
Just then Briscoe began fumbling with every knob and button on the dash and steering column. He looked like a 10-year-old boy feeling a couple of tits for the first time.
"What the fuck are you looking for?" I asked.
"The eject button!" he screamed.

We were in trouble! We passed by the first rest stop; it was closed! We approached another...closed! Our doom had been set in motion and I was certain that if Briscoe was ready to give up a few miles back, then at this point he was prepared to drive us over the cliff just to end it in the name of Rock and Roll.

"What are we going do about this shit, brother?" I asked, trying to ignore my shattered nerves and instill hope into a broken man.

"Wake up Toby and have him get us one of those beers!" Briscoe shouted. "My eyes are shutting down."

"A beer?" I shouted back at him, stuttering like an imbecile who had just spent the day huffing lead based paint. It was at that moment that I achieved a level of clarity. The panic and fear of sudden death had somewhat diminished, and now rather than hang on for dear life, I wanted to let go and ride it out.

There wasn't a Colorado State Patrolman alive insane enough to pull us over during a storm like this. Not only would we not be pulled over, but we were in fact "on our own." The center line had disappeared miles behind us, and from what I could tell, we were either on the interstate, off in the median, or driving off of a goddamned cliff straight to hell. I was in absolute agreement with Briscoe's unspoken theory. If ever there was a good time to booze it up, risking ones life, one mile above sea level was about the best place to do it. We might as well go for it all. Neither of us knew how long we would wearily turtle down I-70 in search of refuge from this "Alaskanese" journey that had sucked us into the center of a world that refused to spit.

"Toby!" I yelled, increasingly annoyed, with hopes that one of them would lift an eyelid just long enough for me to hit them in it without it being considered a sucker punch. "Wake up goddamnit! We're sliding down a fucking mountain!" Neither would budge.

"Maybe he's dead," Briscoe said laughing like a mad scientist who had just discovered how to make herpes terminal.

"Just keep your eyes on the road man." I shouted back. "What eyes?" He replied, laughing even more hysterically, losing his mind just one snowflake at a time.

I knew we were in serious trouble. A winter storm of this magnitude was how people who lived in the Rockies died. At this altitude, diseases like cancer and AIDS could not possibly out kill the state's steep fucking mountains. It was nature's way of keeping a solid check on how much life was allowed to live at one time. Swift winter kills were no strangers to this part of the country. This was everyday life in the mountains. Most of the natives inhabiting this mile high land had figured out how to stay alive while white death claimed the rebellious. We on the other hand, were not as savvy. We were from Southern Indiana. A place where two inches of snow would almost always send people spiraling out of control off of the highway and into a six foot ditch.

The insurance agencies wouldn't even answer the phone on days when snowfall was accounted for throughout the Tri-State. All of them knew they would be filing claims for months on everything from minor fender benders to the totaled out mini-van of the promiscuous soccer mom. If you called, it always seemed that your agent was out of town on vacation and could not be reached until weeks later. The receptionist would usually give a fully exercised spiel. "Mr. Harper is out of town until next Wednesday on vacation, but I can take down your information and have him call you as soon as he gets back." This usually translated into. "Mr. Harper is in Vegas on a serious losing streak, trying to win back embezzled premiums while partaking in prostitutes and cheap whiskey.

Toby finally woke from his sleep through the coldest hell that had ever been seen by man or beast. As I thought about it, we could have been the only survivors. There wasn't a living soul on the road, and the miles behind left truckers and tourists whipping their vehicles into icy graves. We were the last men and lesbian on a sinking ship!

"You fucking missed it, Toby!" I said, shaking my head while searching in an atlas, trying to get an idea where we were and find an open town close to us.

"Yeah, it looks pretty bad out there." he replied.

"My eyes have officially stopped working." Briscoe shouted.

"Do you need me to take over?" Toby asked.

"Are you kidding?" I shouted. "If he stops the van now we might not be able to get this goddamned thing going again... There's fifteen inches of snow out there!"

"I'll be ok," said Briscoe. "Just hand me one of those beers!"

"Me too," I shouted.

"I'm not going to let you drink and drive in my van!" shouted Toby. "Especially while your driving in this shit!"

"It's 3.2 for Pete's sake!" Briscoe shouted. "I'd have to drink the whole entire twelve just to get a buzz."

"I'm not driving," I said. "Let me get one in me to calm me down a little bit."

My knuckles were white from setting up in the passenger seat and gripping the dash. The only time I let go was to fumble with the World Atlas that was informative in regards to direction but not worth much in the event of a massive blizzard.

"None of us are getting any beer until we get to a rest stop," Toby said.

"That could be days!" I shouted.

I couldn't make any sense out of the atlas any more. I was completely spent. My eyes were ravaged and I was rabid with fury. I couldn't believe that there were no open rest areas. It made sense to me that in the event of an emergency, travelers needed somewhere to ride the storm out, a place to get some help, but that wasn't the case. The city seemed to almost turn its back and lock the doors, implying that it was every man for himself whenever the mountains decided to lay their furious hands down.

"It looks like there is an exit around Eagle," Toby said. "Maybe we can find a cheap hotel or something and get out of this mess."

"We don't have the money for a hotel!" shouted Briscoe.

"Well, maybe we can find a nice parking lot somewhere," Toby replied.

"How many more miles is this exit?" Briscoe asked.

Just as they were discussing the exit, I noticed a sign on the side of the highway that read "Eagle 57 miles". The snow had started to taper off a bit and the further we traveled the less snow seemed to be on the ground. "I think we're through the worst of it," I said.

After another hour or so we noticed that we were close to the Eagle, Colorado exit 147. There were no signs of the exit being closed... and had it been, we surely would have tried to get off of it anyway. After all, we were on "the road" and everyone knows that while on the road all of the rules that the normal people of society are forced to follow go straight out the window. You become fearless and overcome by a feeling of invincibility. No law enforcement in his right mind would dare fuck with a no name band shuttling across the United States in a mini-van. "Excuse me sir, but do you know who the fuck you're talking to?"

Minutes before we jumped off of I-70 onto exit 147 Deni woke up even more oblivious than Toby had been an hour or more prior. "Are we still not in Denver?" she asked.

"Girl, you had better thank your lesbian gods that you're not dead right now!" I shouted. "We were just in the biggest fucking blizzard I've ever seen!"

"So where are we?" she asked.

"Almost to an exit in Eagle." replied Briscoe. "I just hope this one is open."

The exit was open, and we wasted no time taking it. The clock now read 3:58am. We had gained more ground by not being able to stop in Denver but added many hours to the overall trip. As we approached the top, we noticed a police officer in his car stationed at the top of the exit. Briscoe rolled down his window and asked the officer if there were any places where we could park and get some sleep. "There is a rest area right over there," the officer said.

It was like a fucking miracle. The rest area was probably only a hundred yards from us. We were safe. Briscoe thanked the officer and proceeded to the rest area. Our time to end the day had gone over due. Our bodies were already shut down and only the zombie form of our bodies were alive enough to push forth into the night. Our weakened bodies had seen the light, and all of us knew exactly what was at the end of the tunnel. Beer!

EAGLE, COLORADO
Punch Drunk With Jack Frost The Ripper

There were only two other cars in the rest area. We had
no reason to make contact with them and didn't.
Especially me. I always expected the worst to happen. I
think I was smart for doing so. You never know who is
going to follow you into a bathroom and ambush you
while you take a piss. The last thing I need, after well
over a thousand miles of travel, is to be raped by some
twisted bastard hiding out, waiting for an opportunity
like this. So I took my car keys and positioned them
between my fingers so that when a fist was made, I had
a sharp bayonet looking object to deal with any fucking
rapist.

After me and Deni used the restroom, Briscoe and Toby
followed suit. It was really goddamned cold and there
were a few inches of snow covering the parking area. I
was wearing a pair of old school cloth "Chuck Taylors".
My feet were not soaked from walking to and from the
bathroom, but they were wet enough to piss me off and
make me uncomfortable. "I've got to change these
goddamned socks," I said to Deni as she dug around in
her bag looking for something. I jumped back in the
passenger seat and turned the van on with the heater
blasting as high as it would possible go. I took my shoes
and socks off and set them on the floorboard to let
them dry.

"Deni can you grab me another pair of socks out of my bag while you're back there?" I asked.

"Which bag is yours?" she asked.

"It's the black duffle bag. Plain black!" I shouted as Deni jumped inside the van while Briscoe and Toby came out of the restroom and headed towards the van.

"I'm fucking exhausted," I said to Deni as she handed me a pair of dry socks.

"I feel pretty good," she replied.

I imagine I would have felt pretty good too if I had been able to sleep through that goddamned blizzard. Not that I was holding that against her. That's just the way it was. She was able to move past the fact that she was packed into a mini-van with three guys, traveling down some strange highway on the way to Los Angeles to play music. She was calm enough to ignore the anxiety and the stress of travel and just go to fucking sleep. I envied her for that. I had been popping sleeping pills since St. Louis and other than a few blackout moments, I couldn't get any rest. Perhaps she had been taking something stronger than what I was taking... maybe if I asked, she would say something like "I've got a prescription for Flexeril that I've been using... do you want one?" That would do wonders for me at this moment. A good old fashion muscle relaxer mixed with a few of those 3.2 beers we had in the back would surely put me down for the night.

"So what are you using to help you sleep so good?" I asked Deni, hoping to get her to admit that she had a

119

special prescription for something good and then offer me one. "Nothing," she replied. "I got too drunk at my friends going away party last night in Bloomington... I needed to sleep."
I rolled down the window and shouted and Briscoe and Toby. "Grab some of those goddamn beers!"
"That's what we're getting right now." Briscoe replied.

The two of them jumped in the van with a cooler full of Kansas 3.2% disguised as beer. Briscoe and I were still apprehensive, but after such a long journey we didn't feel like fighting it anymore. We cracked open can after can until the beer was no more, and all of us were laughing like we were sitting on a short bus on a field trip to the zoo. It was truly insane. We all appeared drunk, but there didn't seem any way possible. Each of us only had a measly three beers a piece, which, in terms of "real beer" consumption, translated into just about one and half beers per person. It wasn't enough to get us buzzed, much less drunk, but there we were - slobbering, laughing uncontrollably, and giving Deni a play-by-play of the battle action we had encountered while in the trenches of the great winter war. As it usually goes, a horrifying event had become a catalyst to some slapstick slice of life.

After an hour of mindless banter, hysterical laughter, and the occasional unexplained boner swelling from my pants, we decided, without conferring with one another, that it was time for sleep. The laughter and conversation was slowing way down and one by one we just started to– cloooose – ouuuur – eyessssss.

It was likely that if we didn't get some rest and get the fuck out of Colorado, we might be trapped in the rest area by another reign of hellish blizzard forcing us into a handful of situations that we may or may not live to regret. One minute you are cutting up with one another and then amidst another night of snow covered doom, a tragedy takes shape in the form of bored out assholes and severed heads. All of us were convicts and imbeciles. Some of us were just better at hiding it than the rest. I didn't trust any of them with my life and I was quite certain that if push came to cannibalism, one of these degenerates would not hesitate to take a bite right out of my ass. Sure we were friends, but people like this are fragile souls. It wouldn't take much to make a lunatic out of any one of them. Especially Briscoe! His wife had warned me a long time ago that although he was kind hearted, that all changed when he was faced with adversity. At that point, he is well prepared to do anything to keep warm, dry, safe, and above all, stay alive.

CAMEO, COLORADO
Gay Johnsons & The Redneck Fashion Retrospective

I felt a shit coming on somewhere back in Kansas, but somehow through all of the chaos of being run out on a rail in Salina, and fighting for dear life through hell frozen over, it had been surpressed, or at least placed at the bottom of the list. Now that we were safely back on I-70, my guts were starting to nag at me again about a little unfinished business that I had been ignoring for about the last five hundred miles.

After an hour and a half of road time, we stopped off at a little roadside gas and grocery in Cameo. A place called Gay Johnsons. The van needed gas, and by now everyone in the van had mentioned needing some kind of breakfast before going much further. It was there that I sent out my first distress signal. I bought a postcard with a photo of the Rocky Mountains on the front of it, along with a stamp, and then wrote home: Near death at 5,000 feet... You can't drive here wearing clown shoes! Note: Haul ass and apply your parking brake at the Denver city limits and skid towards the ocean. Only then will you have a fighting chance..."
I signed it, addressed it to my brother, dropped it in the outgoing mailbox in front of the store, and then went back inside to see what everyone else was up to. Briscoe and Toby Shain were sipping on some coffee and browsing a rack of cheap trucker hats and t-shirts.

The merchandise, most printed with either the phrase of the week in White Trash America or with other sayings that had since the last decade been technically obsolete. Like...

Git-R-Done!

Aint Scared!

Born to be Free!

Save a horse...ride a cowboy!

"You know, if you boys would have been wearing one of those shirts back in Kansas, we wouldn't have had all that trouble." I said.

"Yeah, no kidding," Briscoe replied. "I thought we were going to get killed."

"You two were sitting in fuckin' redneck America, fuckin' with vetrans and shit. What do you expect?" I shouted.

"We weren't fucking with anybody" Briscoe replied. "That bartender had some serious issues."

"Yeah, he wasn't very professional was he?" said Toby.

"Fuck that. It was the best fucking show we've ever done," I replied. "We should be getting kicked out of fuckin' bars like that all of the time."

"Right," Briscoe replied. "We're not that kind of band."

"What kind of band is that?" I asked. "And where in the hell is Deni?"

"I think she's in the van," Toby replied.

"Speaking of van," Briscoe replied, "We really need to get going. Looks like we've got a lot of ground to cover today."

"Yeah, lets get out of here," Toby said. "The girl up

there at the checkout told me we were still about 240 miles from Utah."

"Damn!" Briscoe replied. "That blizzard really was a set back."

"Apparently," Toby replied.

"Well, fuck Colorado!" I shouted. "Let's get the fuck out of this cold ass shit."

"Let's go," Briscoe said. "Do you need anything before we go?"

"Well, I kind of need to take a shit," I replied. "But there is no way in hell I'm going to be able to do that here. I'll just hold it."

We joined Deni in the van and within five minutes we were back on I-70, plowing the downside of Colorado through 245 miles of sunshine and snow, slush, water, and finally some heat.

WELCOME TO UTAH
The Constipation Desert of Sawed Off Mormons

We finally rolled into Utah later that afternoon, passing some wooden signage letting us know that we were in fact "Leaving Colorful Colorado." The shit I had been trying to hold back was now fighting the hell out of my guts, tearing my insides apart, and reminding me of its aggressive presence by shooting some shanking pains into my side.

"Hey man, I'm going to have to take that shit pretty soon." I shouted to the front of the van. "I think it sat in there to long... my body is shutting down!"
"There's a rest area coming up," replied Briscoe. "Will you be able to do it there?"
"I'm going to have to try," I said. "This is killing me."
"We might as well have lunch while we're there," Toby chimed in - "But I don't see any signs of food anywhere."
"I can make everyone a peanut butter and jelly" Deni said. "I've got plenty."

We pulled into the Wayside Rest Area just off the interstate. With the exception of a scenic picnic area overlooking a beautiful mountainous desert, the rest area itself was nothing spectacular. It was basically a place to stretch out a little, enjoy the view, and do things like I was getting ready to do.

"Do you think one of you guys can guard the door while I do this thing?" I asked. "Because if someone walks in, there is no way I'm going to be able to go."

"I'll guard the door." Briscoe shook his head. "Man... You have got some hang-ups!"

"I still don't have anything on you Briscoe!"

The two of us walked towards the restroom while Toby Shain and Deni muscled our cooler to the picnic area at the top of the hill.

"So what are you going to tell them?" I asked.

"Tell who?"

"Anyone who tries to get in here while I'm shitting."

"I'll just ask them to wait a minute. A friend of mine is getting sick in there."

"Yeah, that should work." I said as I made my way to the bathroom.

"Well hurry up!" Briscoe shouted. "I'm ready for lunch."

When I opened the door I was surprised to find two things. First, the toilets did not have full size walls built around them. They were made of bricks and were only about half as tall as most bathroom stalls that I had seen. Second, a man using the shitter in the middle of this Utah brick shithouse was staring directly at me. I nodded at him politely and walked over to the sink to wash my hands. I thought maybe he would finish up and leave before I got through washing up. Instead, I had to keep from making eye contact with him inside the mirror above the sink. I took my time drying my hands and he just kept staring at me... So I left.

"You finished already?" Briscoe asked.

"Fuck no! There's some asshole in there staring at me over the top of the shitter walls!"

"What? How was he doing that?" Briscoe asked. "You seen him?"

"Yeah, from the goddamned shoulders up! The fucking stall walls are sawed off! I almost had a fucking aneurysm in there."

"So what do you want to do?" Briscoe asked.

"I guess I'll hold it awhile longer. Fuckin' shit!" I replied as Briscoe and I walked up the hill to have lunch with Deni and Toby Shain. I wasn't hungry, so I passed on the peanut butter, took of my shirt, and went for a hike. "I'm going for a walk" I said.

"What? So you can shit?" Briscoe asked.

"No, I just want to see what's out here."

"Rattlesnakes are what is out there," Toby shouted, "Maybe even a scorpion or two."

"We're going to need a snakebite kit yet." Briscoe shouted.

I stood at the far edge of the mountain, staring down at the desert below, thinking about how much better I seemed to have it now than I did the year before. And even though I knew it wouldn't last, somehow the desert sold me on it. I took off all my clothes and began looking for some answers where no one else ever thought to look... inside a state of abandonment known as Utah. No services two-hundred miles.

To Be Continued...

Louder Than Hell, the novel... coming soon.

Mike Adams

Residence Inn Mpls Depot
425 South Second Street
Minneapolis MN 55401
612-340-1300

I don't remember having any dreams until I
was about thirteen years old...it was then
that they started and still haunt me to this
day... This particular dream always begins at
dusk, through the eyes of a bird, in a slow
motion flight across a Midwestern desert
into a violent sunset. The color of the
landscape is as sinister as I have ever
seen; its horizon burns these tones of deep
apocolyptis, burning with such a brilliant
dissent, as if purgatory were in Autumn, and
fashionably drenched in kerosene blooms.
It's the kind of bold and seductive image
where secrets lie, secrets way beyond those
printed in Revelations. This dream contained
mysteries of the spiritual hangover; all of
them dangling from the gates, all of those
lost passions of everyone who continues to
live through a promise of new horizons
before ever realizing they have been
condemned to Hell.

This I see from the branch of a Walnut Tree;
a farmer, an old dusted man who I have never
seen anywhere but inside of this dream. He
pulls out an old red handkerchief from his
back pocket and blows a gob of snot and soil
atop of many other layers of his lungs,
folding it one end over the other to wipe
brackish secretions of moonshine off of his

face. Staring into the east, he watches the sun sink slowly into the depths of the most ancient abyss - an articulant image far from Baas and many others who feed from its fire. This I know; beneath his feet was all he had left. His farm once turned the greenest eyes of all envy; baring fifty-five acres of fertility. Every sown seed reaped bountiful harvests. But now, all that remains is rested in crumbling beds of russet abandonment; dehydration. The Susans now lay black-eyed and dying.

Baas' farm had become a barren wasteland; a reflection of a newly sculpted face that could not shroud his hollow soul. He was not unlike most people who once lived prosperous in these parts; for they too had been ripped apart by the acts of their God. Everything within the simple lives of Baas Perter and others in this rural community had been violently revoked; a rapture inside of a world that for most of them, had only just begun. Yet, most were left alone to die, to suffer a multitude of sun strokes that would surely last as long as decades to come before being drown in the scarlet blood pools by the greatest beast.

Mike Adams

THE THREE OF... MCMXXV

It was on the eighteenth day of the third
month of the year, in the thicket of the
darkness when it arrived. The beast was
gargantuantanic; it was a large, fiery,
furious coil, without warning, snapping
Midwestern necks during the hours of those
most dead. It rose above their feeble
slumbers, a giant serpent of black with
charcoal eyes, dust dancing under the last
quarter of the full worm moon. This serpent
had somehow found its way off its Goddamned
belly and discovered fallacies in Eden. It
was unleashed. Tyranny had been set into
motion, pillaging all of Eve's children;
it's an execution, a cutthroat symphony
inside chapter twenty-thee, Revelations.
Whipping its vile stomp of the eternal
damnation brought down from western heavens,
leaves behind only the stench of sacrificial
lambs as its signature. All of the deadest
of the dead laid inbetween the forks of the
beasts tongue, one that would soon torture
survivors with loss, much of it spread
across a vast eastern grave.

Many a life, both young and old, were lost
that night. For many, the darkness that had
come would have no end for the morning after
the sun did not shine. The community had
been rendered helpless, finding itself
buried under the remnants of stick and
stone. Their cries, silent screams, a
beacon's call for all of those lost but not
yet gone. The whitest sheet had been pulled
over the eyes of three states for it was

easier to see the light through cloth, than
to seek life through a darkened room.

On the third day those who remained alive
within the destructed land began to adjust
their focus on the ravaged eastern
landscape. The grey division frighteningly
revealed the magnitude of terror's
continuation. Much of the town laid in
rubbish and ruins. Homes, businesses,
churches and schools, all were devastated.
The ashes of burning relics lay atop mounds
of imploded dwellings; echoes of the
serpents whipping dirge continued to scatter
debris across the coldest, dismal dead of
winter.

This scene, these visions, can only be
revealed in black and white; yet the curse
defined a portrait of morosity through the
superimposition of radical and luminous
terrorcolor, revealing forty blackened
towns, each with flesh and stone corpses,
some in the hundreds, decapitated bodies
draped ornamentally solemn, suspended from
the highest stakes of the naked wood like
puppets left to bleed out on the ground
below their crucifixions. A myriad of
mutilation. There were enough severed limbs
to stack, most filled with shards of
shattered glass and splintered wood; even
more bodies floated in lakes and rivers,
while others remained buried or lying in
ditches and county roads across the bloody
three.

The greatest beast had spanned two hundred
and nineteen miles, killing and devouring

lives west to east. The Black Serpent's ferocious coiling had shown no mercy; it was a percussive obliteration, keeping alive only a chosen few to chronicle its backbiting return.

From the devastation there were not any true survivors. Those who managed to survive were left to suffer beyond any life imaginable in Hell, sentenced to forever mourn the ghosts of love and happiness, trapped inside of yet another poisoned Valhalla. Baas Perter lost his wife and thirteen year old son that night...

THE BEATING & NIGHTMARE CO.

Baas peeled off an old engineers cap, one he had farmed in for many years, while starring into yet another one of days faded lanterns. The cap was drenched in sweat, the sweat of an empty man, a cloth crown stained in scars and thorns. Baas wore it as a reminder, but more than that, as a gateway from his life into the deaths of everyone that ever loved him. The cap, which began as a morbid token of his youth, was the only thing his father ever gave him aside from several severe beatings and an overstuffed pillow of nightmares.

...goddamnit boy!

Wiping the salt from his eyes onto his shirt sleeve, he put the cap back on, looking once more to the west as the sun made its finally dissention into darkness. With his back turned on the east, his weary soul finds a break somewhere within the grips of wood and steel; darkness is now...
There would be no fall harvest this year for there was no crop; even if Baas could have sown the seeds of ten-thousand, a thirsty month like August would have surely claimed the lot, just as the serpent had stricken, fang deep, down upon his family, with hissing breath - reigning venom, claiming everything underneath Baas's old engineers cap. Baas Perters will to remain strong was an illusion; it always was, even before losing all. It was no fault of his own; he was unrightfully tormented by loss, grief

and abandonment in a persevering attempt to simply live, determined to take something back, no matter how small, no matter how…

But that spirit was gone; only wilted echoes remained, slowly driving him into an oblivious Siberian eternity, lying somewhere beneath the deepest chambers of Hell. All but a shell had disintegrated upon waking to first morning light just to bury the treasures forever. The land would be the only thing left. Even as a rotting corpse of prosperity, it would surely survive him.

After the funeral, Baas prayed to the Holy Spirit for strength, the strength to continue in his efforts to rebuild all that was left and salvageable; he prayed for the strength to overcome his hatred and the debilitating struggle in keeping inside of a continued faith in the Lord as a good and merciful God. He prayed for a resurrection of many desires…the ability to continue to live his life even as each passing light fainted further from its spark, absorbing less, and even more, than the ones before it... Baas wanted God to be the good shepherd that his Catholic faith always taught him to be; Baas needed guidance to move past all of the agony embedded inside of the empty that, at one time, contained enough of his heart to remind him that he was still alive. Baas Perter prayed for new beginnings, but his desperation fell short of Samhain.

SARDINE TWIG WHO?

And he that killeth a beast shall make it good; beast for beast
—Leviticus 24:18

A widowers night was now upon him. As the darkness crowned yet another day, the farmer rode the golden ass without contemplating his position within the land of nylon baby rats, and the symmetry in which they entailed. What did it mean to be alive in a time where time does not exist? Was it likely to only be seen by those unseen, the rest left to view through a single dimension, Alone, pairs of black and white eyes that will never be allowed to see the light of day for its truth; blinded by the magicians illusions to only see fear in darkness, and forever remain in such darkness until carefully squinting into the brilliance of the almightily morning star, without becoming too eager to see it all in a day.

Mike Adams

DOCTOR TELEVISION
I:

I know that Doctor Television cannot be
trusted, yet without him I am sure to be
doomed. I've been standing in the middle of
this room having a stroke for what seems
like more than a week now. A pathetic
stroke, that is neither efficient or
sympathetic enough to just get on with
killing me, or at least send seizure signals
to my brain, to leave my family no choice
but to have me put in a nursing home. I
would live the rest of my fucking life lying
around in my own shit and piss while oddly
shaped women with malignant facial
deformities fondle my junk and feed me fruit
cocktail. At thirty-five years old I would
likely be the youngest vegetable man in
captivity, dead alive in a cut rate
facility, where scrawny nigger ex-cons get
third shift nurses spun on rocks and dust,
taking turns getting their faggot on,
running butt-fuck trains on hairy *Hellen
Keller* assholes… while the others find
amusement in jacking off into mashturbated
potatoes.

Goddamnit God! Please don't let this kind of sick shit happen to me. Just fucking kill me alright? Is that not enough to appease your wicked red Goddamned hands? I mean Christ on fucking butcher knife Lord, have-some-fucking mercy... Jesus shit!

My prayers were left unanswered. I continued to stroke out in my living room, my goddamned forearm was tighter-than-ever, my feet as heavy as a pair of concrete moon boots. The smell of death and wonderlust lingered about the room; it reeked of the foul breathe of a skillet seered leper in green onions. Upon further inspection the source of the smell appeared to be coming from my right armpit.
A rogue gang of Below Seventies are on the lam in Southern Indiana tonight after hijacking a yellow Tonka, taking the Kramden (bus driver: Ralph kramden) hostage, and leaving him for dead in a section eight Walmart parking lot.

Docter Television is in cahoots with Paul Nipitz. Neither of them believe the B70's intentionally murdered the Kramden.
- "We do not believe the murder was either premeditated or intentional. Once we locate the suspects we'll have a better understanding of exactly what happend. But at this time we are still conducting our investigating."

I know that Doctor Television cannot be trusted.

Television had no comment...
The threat of a murderous pack of illiterate schitzopaths prowling the Southern Indiana streets scares the hell out of me. Imagine all of the heinous acts of krokus pocus that will erupt if they are not apprehended posthaste. It is no secret that the seed will continue to spread. A revelation that may require our immediate attention.
I'm not convinced that Paul Nipitz isn't associated with the 70's. His voice sounds like that of a dull soldier writing a letter to his father.

Nipitz fears the witchhunt:
A female spokesperson for Doctor Television is in route back to headquarters after a meeting with Paul Nipitz who has returned to the homicide scene. Richard Denver tells him
- "You handle The Doctor like a pro," Nipitz chuckles.
- "Yeah, well, some of them are easier than others."

- "I guess that's why they pay you the big bucks, says Dever with his tightly clinched monotone ass hole."

Paul Nipitz replies, "Shh, big headache is more like it. I'm telling you Denver, we have got to catch these invalids by morning, hell preferably by tonight!"

Denver nods in agreement sticking his hands in his pockets and sighing, "Yep, I think one gang rape by forcible sodomy and a snapped neck is enough for the week."

It is to be considered that this type of villainous outburst of psychosexuality is triggered largely in part by the Sperma Morbus (seed sickness), sperm degeneration most common in the mental mar of those resident to the Midwestern states. Millions of clusterphobic spermentias inside of a terror brawl like Bourbon Street Looters in the grips of the rising flood - This is the true degeneracy theory. Refer to Mr. Harry Clay Sharp, a prison physician in Jeffersonville, Indiana who, in 1899, mandated vasectomies for all inmates. The attention of Sharp's clinical anti-spermentia focuses on his fear of degeneracy due to masturbation, but it is suspected that his treatment was due mostly in part from the signs of the cross eyed and crooked. Indiana has been aware of its position as the American axis for incest, queer, and retardation since 1907, becoming the first state of The United States to endorse a eugenic sterilization law. After three hundred years, the degeneracy is no longer a discounted theory; it is proof. A B70 mongrel with the morbic fever masturbates any time, any place, eatin' his pecker scabs like potato chips, cramming gravel, his thumb, and vegetables up his ass to squeeze the remainder of cum dust from his battered and bruised prostate.

The receptionist announces, "Nim Chimpski, Dr. Anima will see you now". In the office: Dr. Anima, Commielab Research staff Beastichiatrist, looks over a report sent down by Animal Resources, "Management wants me to sort out your perversions. They tell me I need to have you fitted for mittens Sir…Unruly erections, excessive masturbation, anal fingering."

Using sign language Chimpski speaks to Anima, "I always feel funny in the spanker".

Anima makes a note. "When you say you always feel funny; is it like a pain or a tickle"?

"Doc, it feels more like a tingle than a tickle," Chimpski signs. Dr. Anima makes some additional notes on his pad. Chimpski begins getting anxious; he can feel a serious muff thumper coming on.

"Sounds like Testee Tinnitus," Anima concludes gawking

Chimpski's monkey meat doodlebugging the room. "Christ almighty son, Ol' Ludwig's got you by the balls…we'll have to give you your severance".

AMPUTEE JUNKY
The Legend of the Dung Manrikigusari

We were all having the time of our lives until someone dared me to snort the crank off of the amputee's nub. Until then I had done my best to avoid any and all contact with this cracked out trailer park serpent that seemed to follow me around the room without actually having to move. I wouldn't, I couldn't make eye contact — yet I kept on trying for fear she would recognize my behavior, become unnerved and pounce on me like el Chupacabra. To fear her from a distance was hard enough without speculation that a blinding fit of rage from this girl could cause me to blackout and swallow my tongue. For a moment I considered walking straight up to the person responsible for inviting this spectacle and pounding their kidneys into the deepest shade of purple. "Adams, there is only one-way off of this bus" I thought to myself, trying to focus more on the voice inside of my head rather than the deafening music also appearing resonate within my skull. " Listen, just stand up and lay down a furious beating on the backbone of a couple of these tweekers. That is if you want any control. After a blast like that, you'll be able to demand the amputee either be removed or locked in the basement until you're ready to leave." There was a part of me that really believed this spontaneous flurry of violence would do the trick. The other part of me was far too distracted by the paranoid geekers pacing the floor like the marching gestapo, frequently calling out for a sphygmomanometer and the number to nine, one, one.

About an hour had past seeming like only a few minutes. I noticed the room was starting to settle into its own. It wasn't that any of us were on our way down. In fact, it was quite the opposite. Most of the die hards in the room not only knew the weight of the road that we had decided to travel, but were also very good friends with the driver, the cooker, the chemist… the man. The average Southern Indiana cooker sells his shit backed with at least a two hit/three day spun-out-of-your-mind guarantee while the real madmen sell it clean enough to stop the heart of a well bread horse. This was common knowledge for those of us who had climbed the ranks from weekend user to full-blown junky. The beginners always snorted it; those of us who wanted it quicker held it to a flame while the extraordinary used needles to chisel their tombstones. No matter the point of entry, it would be days before any of us would consider rest. Although throughout the years of watching speed hounds like myself, I could see the room was not far from an atmosphere of grandeur combined with cigarette smoke and incessant chatter of grand schemes that would never see the sober light of day.

I opened a bottle of beer I had managed to catch from some guy who randomly tossed them into the living room every time he got one for himself. I took a sip and set the bottle down near the edge of the couch, noticing my left bootlace had become untied for absolutely no reason at all. While messing around with the boot, I considered the possibility of there being a small animal underneath the couch with an over zealous lust for black shoelaces. "This makes the third time tonight" I thought to myself, feeling underneath for anything that might help me understand why. There was nothing within reach that could explain it. I thought about how I could catch the culprit in the act by staring down at my boots long enough to stomp it dead once it returned.

"Is there a ferret in the house?" I asked with both eyes focused on the floor preparing for the worst. I don't remember ever hearing anyone answer me. All I heard was an unknown voice belting out from the sidelines, "Hey Adams, I'll give you five bucks to snort some of this shit off Missy's nub!" The unexpected shouting startled me sending a rapid shot of adrenalin into my heart popping me up like a jack in the box. My face cringed in utter disbelief and embarrassment as I attempted to draw some conclusion as to which one of the scrawny yuppies across the room I was going to kill. At this point a target would be extremely hard to determine. The entire room erupted

into a certain type of hysteria that one
might come to expect from inside a padded
cell - Even Missy, the one armed junkie, was
gasping for air and gripping her gut. I was
the only one in the room who wasn't
laughing. I felt like I was about to be
eaten by an angry mob of starved circus
seals barking and lunging at me for the last
biscuit. It was then that I realized how
much trouble I was about to endure. The
amputee with her impetigo grin rose up
slowly and headed towards me. I felt my
right ear turn red, heating up one side of
my face, forcing me to believe that I was
having a stroke.

Everyone in the room was now cheering as if
in a Roman coliseum, watching the release of
a hungry lion. I stood up and took a few
steps to the left while trying to determine
how to make it stop. The guffaw of wild
hyenas, raucous and mean, had officially
taken over. "You're only making it worse!" I
shouted as the amputee came after me at full
force. "Lady, come on now!" I yelled,
darting into the next room and down the
hall. I fled at high-speed dirt, but she
tailed with such a rabid disposition that it
was clear just how determined she actually
was. "Get this mongrel away from me!" I
cried out in desperation hoping that someone
would show a little mercy and stick a
shotgun slug into the back of my head, but
when I turned to look over my shoulder all I
could see was Missy, untamed and violent,
shaking her nub at me as if trying to get
something off of it. It was frightening. I
could smell the arm. It wreaked of ace

144

bandage and generic oatmeal. There was no way in hell that I would surrender this fight and succumb to this madcap cripple's nub.

The amputee scared me beyond any fear. She was as short as she was round and spoke with a lisp that some had said was caused by accidentally biting off part of her tongue giving out blowjobs for dope. The state had placed her children into foster care months ago because one of them tested positive for methamphetamines during a welfare checkup. She was a friend of a friend of somebody's cousin who hung around with friends of mine. She was an ornament of terror - everyone simply tolerated her presence because no one seemed to have the guts to tell her she wasn't welcome. Some even feared she was a rat working to assist the cops in busting the local dope manufactures as a means to get her kids back quicker. In a garbage can full of junkies, jobless stoners, and maybe even a suspected pedophile, Missy was the rotten banana stuffed inside of an old corpse buried deep at the bottom.

Without much time to think or breathe I ducted into an open bedroom and jumped on top of the bed turning to face the monster as she stormed in after me. "Stay back godamnit!" I shouted doing my best to keep a safe distance. "I'm not snorting anything off that arm of yours." I was holding a pillow in front of me franticly examining the room for a bullwhip. Missy would not speak. The only sound she made was a horrendous laugh followed by a snorting sound as she lunged at me from the floor. In an attempt to fend her off, I brutally swung the pillow with both hands from left to right hoping she would grow tired and give up on me as easily as she did on life. I could still hear the others roaring at the highest imaginable volume and I was now convinced that if I was going to get out of this unscathed, I was going to have to handle it on my own. I took a step back that must have looked as if I was winding up for a fastball, and I delivered a solid crack with the pillow against the side of her head, knocking her to the floor. I thought about jumping on top of Missy's head with both boots and caving in her skull, but decided it was for the best to just get out. I was once again in the hall screaming "If one of you motherfuckers don't get this crazy bitch away from me I'm going to set this whole goddamned house on fire!" It wasn't long after my escape before Missy was in pursuit again. I felt like I was going to be sick. I was out of breath, out of patience and thought my next move might be to turn around and beat the amputee unconscious. I spun around committed with my fist doubled up preparing to throw both arms out of socket beating this hog into a coma. Missy was coming at me fast. "Just one solid blow to the temple and she'll be done for" I

thought to myself. "Just one vicious blow." Missy had gotten just about as close to me as she was going to get before running the risk of being put down, but a piercing screech from behind the bathroom door stopped all of us dead in our tracks. The door flung open, and out come this lanky hick that someone had called Sherm screaming something about an "Indiana Bullwhip."

The riot between Missy and me had lost its momentum now that everyone's attention had shifted to the maniac running at top speed from the shitter. I couldn't remember Sherm ever being in the house, much less the bathroom where he must have been locked away for thirty minutes or more. Now he was out and running, swinging a tube sock around like some strange Japanese Manrikigusari. There was no way of knowing that Sherm had gone completely berzerk other than by the pitch of his war cry as he sprint across the floor towards the crowd. Some thought they were about to be killed, and began diving to the floor without valor, taking cover as if in a grade school tornado drill. I was confused but still sharp enough to react and get away before Sherm smashed the sock across the amputees face sending her to the floor. I watched as he thrashed the amputee unmercifully, leaving the contents of the sock

and horrible stench behind. "Jesus fucking Christ," I yelled over the top of the other screams and cries of disgust amplifying throughout the house. I couldn't believe my eyes. The only thing I was willing to trust was my nose and it was telling me that some dumb hick just horse slapped an amputee with a tube sock full of shit! Everyone was running for the door, even the owner of the house. Nobody knew who was going to be next to make contact with Sherm's "Indiana

Bullwhip," and no one was taking any
chances.

Strangely enough, I didn't budge. I was
frozen and amazed. That lanky bastard had
just executed one of the most diabolical
feats of sheer insanity that had ever been
performed. Sherm was down on all fours
across from the amputee pointing and
laughing with the grimace of a rabid animal
infected with mange. Missy was in a frenzy
flopping around on the floor trying to get
the bullwhip bomb out of her eyes and off of
her lips. Her cries were so loud that I got
the impression she must have been in
excruciating pain. The intensity of her
actions ravaged her ability to properly
communicate, worsening her lisp, rendering
most of everything she yelled beyond
comprehension. I only understood her when
she said "you son of a bitch" and "in my
mouth" because that was how she ended most
of her exclamations, heavily emphasizing
each word every single time. But no matter
how loud she screamed, her spit just didn't
go the same distance as her grim flailing
about the room. She looked like a tortured
fish. I caught myself thinking, "How many
times in my thirty-three years have I bared
witness to some redneck imbecile wailing on
a great American reject with a tube sock
full of dung?" "And whose sock was that
anyway?" I took a quick look at Sherm's feet
and he still appeared to have both of his
socks and shoes on. But then I thought, "why
am I still here?" I was the third wheel in a
crap match between a junky amputee and a
hick who had obviously sunken into the early

stages of syphilis. I noticed that the music that had been rattling around in my head was no longer there. Now I felt like a sicko, as the last witness to one of the few violent bowel movements involving two people. The laughter had begun to die out and, from where I was standing, that which appeared to be over had only just begun.

I finished the beer I had left sitting beside the couch but not before examining it for remnants of bullwhip shit. I thought about how Sherm got the shit into the sock. "Did he pick it up and put it in to the sock?" "Did he actually hold the opening of the sock up to his ass and squeeze a load into it?" "Why?" I tossed the empty bottle on the couch walking past Missy and Sherm on the way out. "Missy" I said. "That's what you get for acting like a fucking animal". I looked down at her lying on the floor. She was too emotional to even look at me, much less reply - so I left. There was a part of me that felt sorry for her, even after she chased me down. I was thankful Sherm did what he did. Otherwise I might have snapped into pieces and killed her.

When I stepped outside everyone was looking on in horror. The man that owned the house was stuck inside a livid rant about beating the hell out of Sherm as soon as he came outside. I warned them that it was best to not go in there for a while. It was just too weird. Then I left.

A few days later I spotted Sherm and Missy drinking together at the tavern. We made

brief eye contact, but never said a word.
"Brilliant" I thought. "Shit covered amputee
meets snaggle tooth redneck." It didn't
surprise me. Although I was somewhat curious
as to how their union transpired, I simply
didn't have the stomach to ask. After the
waitress brought me a beer, I sat there
drinking with confidence and pondering my
supposed epitaph. Here lies Mike Adams. A
man who vowed never to snort anything off of
a stump that used to wiggle and hold shit. A
relentless soul existing all of his days
without sexing up anything covered in toilet
bowl soup.

The Holy Sh*t

8813483R0

Made in the USA
Charleston, SC
16 July 2011